W9-BWE-304

3 4604 9101879898

j Dal
Daley, Michael J.

Space station rat

WITHDRAWN

SPACE STATION

RAT

SPACE STATION

RAT

MICHAEL J. DALEY

Holiday House / New York

SALINE DISTRICT LIBRARY
555 N. Maple Road
Saline, MI 48176

OCT 2005

Acknowledgments

I wish to thank all the members of the Monday night writers' group for their invaluable critique and support; especially Jeanne Walsh for her attention to the fidelity of Rat's voice, and Seth Wheeler for teaching me to run on a space station. Also, thanks to my editor, Regina Griffin, who loves Rat as much as I do, and my agent, Nancy Gallt, who persisted in handling *Space Station Rat* despite a certain aversion to rodents.

Copyright © 2005 by Michael J. Daley
All Rights Reserved
Printed in the United States of America
www.holidayhouse.com
First Edition
1   3   5   7   9   10   8   6   4   2

Library of Congress Cataloging-in-Publication Data
Daley, Michael J.
Space station rat / by Michael J. Daley.—1st ed.
p. cm.
Summary: A lavender rat that has escaped from a laboratory,
and a lonely boy whose parents are scientists, meet on an
orbiting space station, communicate by e-mail, and ultimately
find themselves in need of each other's help and friendship.
ISBN 0-8234-1866-9 (hardcover)
[1. Space stations—Fiction. 2. Rats—Fiction. 3. Science fiction] I. Title.
PZ7.D15265Sp 2005
[Fic]—dc22   2004040534

For Jessie Haas,
who knew the liverwurst had to matter,
and Lenore Blegvad,
who knows the sound of leaves

CONTENTS

SPACE STATION

CHAPTER ONE

Rat

Rat did not know which was worse: being hungry most of the time, or being lonely all of the time.

She huddled in the shadows just inside the air vent. Through the grate she could see into the cafeteria. Alone in the large room, the boy sat at a table, eating an apple. He got it from one of the machines on the wall.

Wicked machines. They gave food to everyone, except Rat. Rat hated them.

The boy ate the apple. Rat heard every bite: the pop of skin, the crush of sweet, white flesh, the wet slurp of juice. The air was heavy with apple smell.

Rat's belly ached with wanting the apple. She bit into a nearby wire to stay calm.

One . . . two . . . three tiny nips with her long, very sharp front teeth. She did not allow herself any more. She did not bite deep. She only grazed the toothsome outer cover.

On a space station, every wire mattered.

A space station was a serious place. It was a clean place. It was no place for Rat.

Rat wondered again at her bad luck. When she escaped from the cage, with the scientists and machines hunting her, there was no time to read labels. She'd hidden in the first crate she found. And so she got blasted into space. A dodge right instead of left, and she might still be on Earth. She might be living outdoors with her wild-rat cousins. She might have interesting-smelling dirt between her toes. She might be nibbling corn in a giant field.

Closer and closer the boy came to the part of the apple he would not eat. Rat did not understand. People never ate that part. A mystery, but lucky for Rat. Sometimes they left that part on the table and went away, the boy more often than anyone else. He was untidy, and left crumbs and toys where they should not be. The boy was often in trouble for these bad habits. Lucky for Rat—sometimes.

Closer and closer. The wire was getting too thin to bite. Rat danced an impatient dance—left paw, right paw, swish of tail.

The boy put the apple on the table.

Rat stopped dancing.

The boy just sat.

Go! Rat could see the white on the apple turning brown. Go! Go!

Nanny came into the cafeteria. Rat cringed into the shadow. Silent. Still.

Nanny was nearly as tall as the boy and shaped like a barrel in the middle. Stuck on top of the barrel section like the lid of a pot was the black disc-shaped head with its one green eye. Pink foam padding—held in place with duct tape—covered the two gripper arms. This robot was not perfect like the others on the space station. It looked unfinished, like one of the scientists' experiments. The gray tape made it seem that way. They used a lot of that tape in the lab.

The robot's glowing green eye swiveled to stare at the boy.

"Tsk tsk tsk tsk," Nanny chirped. "You are five minutes late for family time."

"So?" The boy shrugged.

"You will make your parents unhappy."

"No I won't. I could be an hour late, and they wouldn't care. They'd be glad. More time to talk sunspots!"

"Tut tut. That is no way for a little boy to speak of his parents."

"It's true!" the boy shouted. He stood up so fast the chair tipped over. "Spots spots spots!!"

He ran out of the cafeteria.

The apple lay forgotten on the table.

Though every muscle tensed for action, Rat dared not move while Nanny remained.

The robot might look dumpy, but its senses were much more like Rat's. They were *better* than Rat's.

The glowing green eye surveyed the mess.

"Tsk tsk tsk," Nanny chirped, then whizzed off after the boy.

Hurry! Or she might not beat the gobbler.

But Rat forced herself to stay still a bit longer. Listen. She heard the *scritch-rip* of the boy's Velcro boots fading as he ran. She heard the whir of Nanny's motor grow faint as it followed the boy. That was all. Rat *loved* those boots! Everyone on the space station wore them. Everyone made noise when they moved. Rat could never be caught by surprise. Not, at least, by a human.

The vent was hinged on top. Two plastic clips held the bottom shut. Even though Rat used this vent often, she always put the clips back on. She did not want the fix-it robots to get suspicious. She grasped the first clip with both front paws, and braced her back legs against the sidewall. She pushed. The first clip slid off, then the second. Lucky for Rat: no screws.

Rat lowered herself onto a pipe on the wall below the vent. The grate slid heavy against her back. She held it open with her hind foot. She flicked her tail out so that it would not get pinched. Just as the grate clacked shut, a door opened in the ceiling above the table and a thick hose dropped down. Chompers and slurpers were on the end of it.

Rat made a wild slide to the floor and dashed across. She jumped to the tabletop.

Bite!

Snap! The gobbler's steely jaw got the other end of the apple core. Rat looked into the black hole of its dark mouth. She pulled and twisted and gulped for air.

The apple core broke. With a mushy slurp, part of it was vacuumed up by the gobbler. But Rat got the biggest piece. She ran. The gobbler snuffled and sponged at the sticky places, then set the chair back on its legs. Safe in the air vent, Rat devoured her prize. But it wasn't enough. It was never enough.

Rat put the clips back on the bottom of the vent. She stared at the empty, spotlessly clean cafeteria. Not even a bread crumb in a corner.

Itch.

Rat licked the scab on her right shoulder. She tasted more new skin, less crusty scab. Almost healed. Just before escaping her cage, Rat did that to herself. She chewed through her own skin. She bit out the rice-sized SeekChip tracker the scientists put into every lab animal.

Wicked scientists!

They taught Rat about skyscrapers and security alarms and ventilation systems; how to find computer rooms and vaults and executive boardrooms. But nothing about space stations. Nothing about food machines. She was supposed to carry food in a body pack when on missions, along with spy tools and weapons. The pea-sized food pellets tasted terrible, but each one was crammed with a whole day's nutritional needs.

Rat had planned carefully. She had made sure she could steal a body pack when she escaped. She had torn the communications gear from the body pack. Even without the SeekChip in her shoulder, without the radio, one of the terrible wheeled jaws had found her.

Lucky for Rat, the sniffer's teeth had sunk into the body pack instead of her. She'd popped the catches, slipped out of the pack, and gotten away. Fleeing the bewildered robot, she had turned the wrong way. . . .

Rat looked through the grate at the sealed metal faces of the food machines. She needed her tools in this place, but all she'd escaped with was her life and her wits.

CHAPTER TWO

JEFF

Scritch-rip! Scritch-rip!

Running drove the bad thoughts from Jeff's head.

Scritch-rip! Scritch-rip!

Running almost pushed the bad feelings from his heart.

Scritch-rip! Scritch-rip!

Run, and the trying-to-be-good got left behind.

Running on a space station was not easy. To run without getting dizzy, or staggering, required all his attention. That's why Jeff did it so much.

Just walking around on a space station was hard enough for most people. It felt like walking on a moving train—an odd sense, as you lifted your foot, that your body was not going to go where you wanted it to. It made some people sick. But not Jeff. He loved the feeling. He spent hours mastering it.

Too-big boots made it even harder. Mom hadn't forgotten a single thing for the project, but she'd left Jeff's special boots sitting side by side in the front hall.

He zigzagged a little as that bitter, disappointed thought spiked into his head. With that loss of concentration came a loss of balance. The tangled maze of rainbow-colored piping on the curved walls blurred. Dizziness threatened. Jeff pushed through it, seeking the sweet spot of no thought and perfect balance.

His vision cleared. There was the captain, dead ahead, his fat body nearly blocking the corridor. He bellowed, "Stop that running at once!"

Jeff braced his legs. The Velcro boots seized the carpet and his feet slid in their looseness. He stumbled onto his hands and knees. The quick change felt like going over the top on a roller coaster. A sick feeling churned his stomach. He stared at the carpet, sure his face was as red as the red stripe showing the way to the toilets. Usually it was okay to run around Ring 9. The captain did not like being in high-gravity parts of the space station. It made him feel his weight. It made him grumpy.

"Where's the fire, huh?"

"Boots're too big." Jeff shifted into a squat and yanked the straps as tight as they would go.

"That's no excuse for running, is it? What if I was carrying acid and you ran into me? It's dangerous, running."

What could he say?

"Where's your emergency mask?"

Jeff patted his hip. The space station was under meteor alert. He was supposed to carry the emergency oxygen mask in case a meteor punctured the station. "I had it a minute ago. It must have fallen off."

"While you were running. Another reason not to."

Jeff had to agree. Meteors made him nervous. They reminded him that black space, empty and deadly, waited just on the other side of the walls.

Meteors traveled so fast that one the size of a marble could punch a hole in the space station's outer wall. Smaller ones just bounced off, but they jiggled things. That really upset Jeff's parents. They needed everything steady for their experiments.

Meteors bigger than a softball never hit the station. They were targeted and destroyed by the trackers before they could. The trackers couldn't detect meteors between marble- and softball-sized soon enough. These were the most dangerous. Nanny told him there was nothing to fear. Nanny could fix any damage. But Jeff hadn't stopped worrying. Who would believe a robot tinkered together with pink foam and duct tape?

The captain crossed his arms. He looked at Jeff. "Got too much fizz for a place like this, that's what I think."

He didn't sound mad. Almost like he understood what Jeff might be feeling. Jeff acted on this possibility quickly, bravely.

"If only I had something to *do*! Nanny just hauls me from lessons to exercises; and I only see Mom and Dad for a bit, and they hardly pay attention. Nanny doesn't even know how to play any *games*!"

Jeff heard Nanny's motor.

The captain glanced over Jeff's shoulder. He lowered his voice, as if he didn't want Nanny to hear. "Well, yes, Nanny is a bit short on programming for that. We've never had a boy here before, you realize. Most jobs are, well, delicate. But I'll think about it. Meantime, carry on—at a walk!"

Jeff flinched. The captain barked that last bit in his usual grump. Then he grabbed the rung of a ladder. Like a blimp, he rose *in* through the ceiling tunnel to the next ring. *In* was closer to the center. Less gravity.

He'll be happier, Jeff thought. He'll forget all about me.

Nanny glided to a stop next to him. Jeff's emergency mask dangled from a gripper. He clipped it to his belt.

"Messy boy! Always dropping your things. Always angering the captain. They will reprogram me if you do not behave." Nanny snatched his right arm in a gripper and tugged him along. "We are late! Walk walk walk."

Jeff tried to resist, but Nanny's grip on his arm was very strong. It worried Jeff, that strength. It didn't seem necessary in a machine thrown together just to keep one unwanted twelve-year-old boy out of trouble.

In the recreation room, Mom and Dad stood with their heads bent together, studying a poster-sized photograph. Jeff glimpsed bright sunshine surrounding a feathery blackness on the image.

"I told you—spots!" Jeff stuck his tongue out at Nanny, then ran to his parents. He pushed between them. "I'm here!"

With a little sigh, they stepped apart. Mom frowned down at him, her mouth as tight as Nanny's gripper. Dad did not seem to see him at first; then he said, "Hey! Hug!"

Jeff held back. "How far have you read?"

"No chapters, no hugs, huh?" Dad laughed, but he looked guilty. Dad was supposed to be reading the EVA Training Manual. They were supposed to be preparing for a space walk together. That's why Jeff had come along. The big adventure . . . bigger than blastoff, bigger than living on a space station, big enough to make all his friends envious when he returned to Earth.

"Can't we do some simulator training, at least?" Jeff asked.

Dad glanced at Mom. Jeff hated that glance.

Mom said, "Really, Jeff, your father simply doesn't have time."

"You said that yesterday. And the day before! And the—"

"Watch that temper," Mom snapped. She took a deep breath. "I'm sorry to be harsh, Jeff. This meteor warning has really put me on edge. You know we didn't plan it this way."

Jeff did know. That's why he tried so hard. But it had been weeks and weeks since they had come here.

Dad usually had lots of spare time. He only helped Mom with the computer work. But Professor Krosta had gotten sick and couldn't come, so now Mom needed Dad to do Professor Krosta's work, too, or the project would fail. That could mean disaster for Earth.

"Mom and I are up against it, Jeff, no doubt. This calculation still won't come out right"—Dad smacked the sunspot photo, and Jeff noticed the long lines of equations his parents had written all over it—"and the heliospectrometer keeps slipping out of calibration."

That was serious. Mom studied sunspots to find out about the sun's energy cycle. "Light is the sun's messenger," Mom liked to say, "and my job is to translate the language." The heliospectrometer let her read the message by analyzing the sun's light. It was the first step.

"The captain promised me it was a world-class instrument," Mom said.

With a glance at Nanny, Dad said, "I'm not sure much is world-class on this space station."

Mom deserved better. The project was important enough. Back on Earth, scientists were about to begin the Global Cooling Initiative, but Mom was afraid they were using the wrong theory—that instead of reversing global warming, they might trigger an ice age. But Mom's theory was ignored by the institutes, universities, and journals. Money didn't come her way as it did for other scientists. That's why they hadn't been able to hire a replacement for Professor Krosta.

Mom said, "I need you to be independent a bit longer, Jeff. There's less than a week to solar maximum. Once we've got the data, Dad will have more time. Maybe we can even stretch the visit a little, to make up for cheating you."

Here. Now. With Mom actually thinking about him even though she was worried about all that might go wrong, Jeff felt he could do what she asked. But he hesitated to promise.

"I must report," Nanny said into the silence. "The boy has irritated the captain."

Jeff wanted to kick Nanny.

"Oh Jeff!" Dad sank to his knees. He held both of Jeff's arms. Worry ridges went up under his whisker-short hair. "You mustn't annoy the captain. He'll make trouble for our work!"

"But I didn't. I wasn't. I mean, we talked!"

"No one can talk to that man," Mom said. "Nanny, full behavior report."

A paper slid out of Nanny's middle, listing all the details of his life since the last family time.

"No!" Jeff grabbed it and crumpled it into a tight ball. Nanny made a little stuttery "tsk." "It was Nanny's fault! Nanny came late. I had to run."

"Naughty naughty boy." Nanny moved between Jeff and Mom. Startled, Mom took a step back. She bumped up against the table. "For the record, ma'am."

Another sheet of paper slid out. Before Jeff could get it, a gripper snapped, catching his wrist. Jeff pulled. It hurt. He clenched his teeth and pulled again. Nanny rocked on her rollers. Sheet after sheet of paper slid out.

"Jeff! Stop!" Mom said.

Jeff stopped. Nanny let go. Mom picked up the report from the floor.

"You should believe *me*," Jeff said. He rubbed at the square-edged dents the gripper had left in his skin.

"Robots don't tell fibs," Mom said.

"Thank you, ma'am," Nanny chirped.

More chirps. But these came from Mom's beeper. She dropped the report, snatching the beeper from her belt to read the message.

"A development!" she said. Mom and Dad strode toward the door. They didn't run. They *couldn't* run. A fast waddle was tops. They hadn't taken the time to learn.

"Study time," Nanny said.

Jeff turned on the robot. "They should believe me!"

The glowing green eye stared at him.

"Study time."

"Not yet!"

Jeff leaped onto the couches and chairs, scattered cushions onto the floor, pushed magazines off the tables, and ripped up the sunspot photograph. Then he ran out of the room.

Nanny's head rotated all the way around. "Dear dear dear."

Gobblers came out of the ceiling. They put everything back in order. They sucked up Nanny's papers. But they left the torn bits of photograph because Nanny told them to.

CHAPTER THREE
STUDY TIME

Rat was on time. So where was the boy? Rat did not like the boy to waste study time. Rat needed to learn a lot to survive on the space station.

She had already learned how lucky she was to be alive. The roar and the squeezing and the floating had been the blastoff of a space shuttle. The enormous open space, with men and nosy robots scurrying and the huge ship hissing in the center of it, had been the landing area of the space station. A very dangerous place for Rat. But she escaped. She found the air tunnels, like the one she was in now. It ended at a vent near the ceiling above the boy's bed. Perfect for observing.

At first Rat thought she could just go

back to Earth. But the boy studied space shuttles. Scary things. There was only one safe place to be. The crate she hid in had been put in that part. If it had gone with the regular cargo . . . well, Rat would be a dead rat. Going back would be complicated. She could not be half-starved and hope to succeed. Besides, there had to be a ship. None had come here since the one bringing her crate and the boy.

Where *was* he?

Patience, Rat told herself. The boy's bad habits often meant food.

Food would be nice.

Rat sat up on her back legs, kinking her tail just right for balance. She groomed her elegant nose whiskers, then licked between her clean, pink toes. Not even a bit of sticky apple juice was left. Rat's front paws drooped. She swayed, nearly tumbling, as her tail went limp. Rat snapped herself to attention.

Bother! She rubbed her pink knuckles hard over her eyes. Do something!

Rat checked the telescope. The telescope let her see across the room to the computer screen. The boy slouched when he studied, so his big head was not in the way. Another bad habit that was lucky for Rat.

Rat had built the telescope from two lenses, a toilet-paper tube, and some gum the boy had stuck under a table. They blamed the boy for the missing lenses. Too bad.

But it had not been the boy who had left half a bologna sandwich in the lab that day, right next to the lenses. What a double lucky day that had been! Rat remembered the tangy taste of mustard—how it made her nose tingle!—and the bread, crusty on the outside, wet-mushy inside, and the meat! The meat!

Rat sniffed hard, trying to bring back all the good smells. But it had been a long time ago.

She checked the aim of the telescope, then gave it a small nudge. When she peered in again, a shadow flashed by, a door slammed, and bed springs jounced. Rat pulled away from the grate. She must not let her nose, or a whisker, or the tip of her tail poke out because the boy often returned from family time upset. He would lie on the bed right beneath the vent, his arms jammed under his head, staring at the ceiling with angry, intense eyes.

There was a knock on the door.

"Go away!" Despite the boy's command, the door opened. Rat smelled still-warm, bittersweet, chewy chocolate chips. Crumbs!

"It is study time," Nanny said. "I have some milk and cookies for you."

"Go away!"

"I am not programmed to go away," Nanny said. "I am programmed to bring you milk and cookies at study time and tell you what lesson—"

"Oh, enough already." Boots thumped on the floor and *scritched* to the door. Rat peeked. The boy snatched the tray from

Nanny. The milk sloshed, and a few cookies slipped off and broke on the deck. A tidal wave of more intense smells rolled into the air vent.

"Hasty hasty," Nanny said.

A small gobbler popped out of a wall tube in the corridor. It skittered around Nanny's rollers, sucking up the spots of milk and crunching the crumbs, leaving a neat line of crumbs just inside the door. It did not come into the room. Except in an emergency, robots were not allowed in private spaces, not even Nanny.

Nanny said, "Study the food machines today. Then you will understand why you should not spill your milk."

Nanny shut the door.

Yes, thought Rat, yes yes yes. Study the wicked machines! Study now!

But the boy did not study. He carried the tray to the computer table. He ate some cookies. Rat watched where every crumb fell. The boy played a game. Then he checked his e-mail. No mail. He used to get e-mail. But one by one his friends stopped writing when something called "camp" got them. At first the boy lied about his wonderful adventures on the space station. Later he admitted that he wished he was at camp with them instead.

Rat wanted to be somewhere else, too.

Study!

Keys clicked. Rat went to the telescope. She gnashed her teeth. It was only the EVA Training Manual. He studied that over and over. But what good was it to Rat?

"Oh, what's the use?" The boy moaned and laid his head down on the desk.

Rat wanted to jump down and bite him! She wanted to use some of the scientists' tools on him. The nice ones, or the nasty ones, she didn't care. Just so she could make him study.

Rat ran far back into the air vent. She found a big, thick, black wire. *Chew-chew-chew*. Black bits piled up around her like chocolate chips. She felt a tingle in her teeth. She felt a tickle in her nose. She smelled copper wire. Rat made herself stop chewing. She picked black bits off her whiskers and groomed them out of her fur. Then she went back to her telescope.

The boy was gone for exercise time. Rat removed the plastic clips and pushed against the grate. For a second Rat clung to the outside of the grate, pretending: I am a gobbler!

Then she dropped onto the bed.

Rat feasted. She ate all the crumbs first. Then she drank milk until she sloshed. What a prize, this wet, warmish milk! To-day, at least, Rat would not have to lick ice off the air-conditioning coils. That hurt her tongue, but she hadn't found water any-where else.

Three whole cookies were left on the tray by the computer. She carried them into the air vent for later. Tricky, not to bite the cook-ies too hard. At least the climb to the vent was easy—up book shelves and cubbies stacked like steps. Before taking the last cookie, she studied the computer screen.

SORRY, NO MAIL.

Rat wished she could find the lesson, but there was a password that only the boy knew. Only the boy, studying, could help her learn. The scientists had taught Rat a lot about computers, but she escaped before learning how to hack passwords.

Rat looked at the message again.

SORRY, NO MAIL.

She could change that!

Rat jumped onto the keyboard. Using all four paws and her tail, she danced on the slightly sticky keys. She wrote a macro virus and put it in the e-mail start-up routine. Now she could type e-mails that looked like they came from Earth.

Why did she know how to do this? The scientists never completely explained. Sometimes they mentioned stealing information, plans, formulas. Sometimes they spoke about destroying these things. Services required by the client. Her training had not progressed far enough for her to need the details.

She was her own client now.

But she could not simply ask about the food machines. She needed a trick. Rat thought a moment, then began her first message. When she was done, the screen read:

To: Jeff@spotseeker.orbit
From: newfriend@home.earth
Subject: Pen Pal

Hi! I am looking for a pen pal who lives in an unusual place. Your address seems unusual. Do you live in an unusual place? Are you looking for a pen pal? Write back.
P.S. Do you like peanut butter???

Chapter Four

Pen Pals

To: newfriend@home.earth
From: Jeff@spotseeker.orbit
Subject: Re: Pen Pal

YES! and YES!
YES! I live on a space station. How's that for unusual? YES! I want a pen pal. Do you really want me for a pen pal? I hope a space station is unusual enough. Please write back right away!!!!!!!
And oh YES!!! I love peanut butter, chunky.

The boy clicked SEND. He jumped out of his chair as if he'd launched a rocket. He whooped and danced around the room. When he sat back down, he played games.

He jiggled. He checked his e-mail every ten minutes. Rat could only answer when the boy went away. She watched all this foolishness with a slow, tense grinding of her front teeth.

Study! Rat could wish, but it was not going to be as easy as that.

Eventually the boy would go to bed right under the air vent. When? Rat did not bother to wait. She curled up next to the telescope. It was not as comfortable as her nest, not as secret, not as safe. But Rat must be here when the boy went away to breakfast.

To: Jeff@spotseeker.orbit
From: newfriend@home.earth
Subject: Re: Pen Pal

A space station is very unusual. What is it like? Do you walk on the ceiling? What do you eat? I'm glad you want a pen pal.

The boy came back from breakfast. He carried a plate of crackers with peanut butter on them. He munched them while he typed. Rat hoped he would not eat all the crackers.

To: newfriend@home.earth
From: Jeff@spotseeker.orbit
Subject: YOU WROTE BACK!!!!!

Hi again. You took so long. I worried I flunked unusual. We walk on the floor. Deck, we call it. The space station is like a big doughnut. There are ten rings around the center. I live on #9. I guess if the station was on Earth, you'd think we walked on the walls. But there is no down or up here. We have *in* and *out*. Because of the spin. Have you ever spun a rope with a knot on the end? That's fake gravity. My mom says, "The earth *hugs* you, but a space station *catches* you." It's not as nice as real gravity. What's your name?

That explains a lot, Rat thought. The scientists put animals into a spinning machine in the laboratory. Not Rat, though. The machine was noisy. It often made them sick. Now she lived in a spinning machine! No wonder her first days were full of bad bumps, as if her legs forgot how to walk. And her tail moved in so many strange, new ways.

The boy left for morning exercises. As Rat dropped from the vent, she thought, I am not going down, I am going out. Rat ate the last cracker and licked the plate clean. She typed:

To: Jeff@spotseeker.orbit
From: newfriend@home.earth
Subject: Re: YOU WROTE BACK!!!!!

I am slow writing. Don't worry if answers take time. I am your pen pal now. But are we really spinning on the end of a rope? Isn't that

noisy? Don't you get sick? I love Swiss cheese.
Can you get that in space?

The peanut butter made her thirsty. Too
bad there was no milk. Rat went to find
some ice to lick. The boy had come and
gone by the time Rat returned.

To: newfriend@home.earth
From: Jeff@spotseeker.orbit
Subject: no rope

Silly! There is no rope. That was an analogy.
And there can't be noise in space. Outside is a
vacuum—just black without air. Sometimes I
worry about the black getting in. This place is
so old, it creaks!!
I have a space suit. I know how to put it on.
It's like trying to get into two snowsuits at
once! My dad and I are going to do a space
walk sometime.

Hey! Do you have snow where you live? I used to go sledding all the time.
You forgot to say your name.

The boy forgot to answer about Swiss cheese, too. But he brought a cheese sandwich the next time he checked his mail, so Rat did get her answer.

To: Jeff@spotseeker.orbit
From: newfriend@home.earth
Subject: no snow

Sledding sounds fun. Creaking is scary. I don't have a space suit or a snowsuit. I have never been outside in all my life. I want to feel grass between my toes someday.

To: newfriend@home.earth
From: Jeff@spotseeker.orbit
Subject: WEIRD!

How come you've never been outdoors? Are you in prison? Is that why you won't tell me your name? I don't think I can write anymore if you are in prison.

To: Jeff@spotseeker.orbit
From: newfriend@home.earth
Subject: Re: WEIRD!

I am *not* in prison. I am *free.* I am unusual, that's all. Please keep writing. I like having a pen pal.
My favorite food is liverwurst.

To: newfriend@home.earth
From: Jeff@spotseeker.orbit
Subject: sorry

Liverwurst—*yuck!* Chocolate for me!
Sorry I made you mad. I like having a pen pal, too. Here is my picture. Can you send me your picture?

Rat did not need the boy's picture. She could see him in person, with chocolate smeared on his face. Rat relaxed. She had not been careful. She had told too much truth. But the boy was willing to ignore the strangeness. Lucky for Rat.

When Nanny took the boy to family time, Rat went to work with the painting program on the computer. She mixed Windsor violet, cobalt blue, and alizarin crimson in a square color block. She pressed her paw against the screen, comparing the color of her fur to the square. It needed some lemon yellow. She adjusted the tint and hue, and added a little Payne's gray. Good enough. Too bad she did not know how to capture the wonderful sheen of the living hairs. She pasted the color square in a new e-mail and typed:

To: Jeff@spotseeker.orbit
From: newfriend@home.earth
Subject: no picture

I cannot send my picture. But I am very
beautiful. I have a lavender coat with white
cuffs. Here is how it looks.

To: newfriend@home.earth
From: Jeff@spotseeker.orbit
Subject: Are you a girl?

To: Jeff@spotseeker.orbit
From: newfriend@home.earth
Subject: no

To: newfriend@home.earth
From: Jeff@spotseeker.orbit
Subject: silly

Well, boys aren't beautiful, silly. Boys are
handsome.

To: Jeff@spotseeker.orbit
From: newfriend@home.earth
Subject: maybe

Maybe. But *I* am beautiful!

To: newfriend@home.earth
From: Jeff@spotseeker.orbit
Subject: FAT

You should see the captain. He's not handsome or beautiful. He's *fat*! I'll never get fat.
I have to exercise four times a day. No one
else has to. I am in the way, that's why. They
would keep me in the gym all day if they
could! Remember *in* and *out*? All the way *in*,
at the very center, there's no gravity. The
zero-g room is there. I can fly and do all
kinds of flips and things. It's like bouncing
off a trampoline, but you never come down!!
I would stay in the zero-g room all day, but
NO, that's not allowed. Too much fun!

To: Jeff@spotseeker.orbit
From: newfriend@home.earth
Subject: scientists are not nice

Scientists are not nice. I speak from experience.

To: newfriend@home.earth
From: Jeff@spotseeker.orbit
Subject: Re: scientists are not nice

I *agree*! I was trying to play chess (do you?) with my dad today. Mom kept bothering him with p factors and 1q angles, then he moved his knight *wrong*! He thought I cheated!

To: Jeff@spotseeker.orbit
From: newfriend@home.earth
Subject: knights

I never move my knight wrong.

To: newfriend@home.earth
From: Jeff@spotseeker.orbit
Subject: let's play!

Let's set up a remote game! That'd be fun.
Of course, best fun if you visited.
We could have fun here, I think. This is an old
space station. It is like a big house with dozens
and dozens of rooms. Bits stick way out from
center, like towers.
I'm not allowed to go exploring. Many places
have not been used, like forever. The lights
don't work. Some don't have air anymore. I
just know it would be fun to go exploring.
Maybe if you came, they'd let us go together.

To: Jeff@spotseeker.orbit
From: newfriend@home.earth
Subject: things we could do

We could find where the food is grown.
Maybe there would be grass.

To: newfriend@home.earth
From: Jeff@spotseeker.orbit
Subject: no grass

We don't *grow* food here. I'm not sure where it comes from, but it is not grown. I will find out for you. Sorry about the grass.

Rat pressed her eye more tightly to the telescope. The tip of her tail quivered. The boy sent his e-mail, then called up the study program. At last! The secrets of the food machines appeared on the screen.

CHAPTER FIVE

Rat Makes a Mistake

Rat was fat. She could not reach an itch at the bottom of her tail. She rubbed the itchy spot against the warm pipe, then sat down to groom her big, round belly. There were crumbs scattered around Rat. Imagine! Too full to eat every crumb! Rat liked that.

Rat was in her nest in one of the forgotten parts of the space station. It was dim and musty-smelling and safe. There was the nice warm pipe, and even some dust. Every once in a while, something made a sound. *Pffss-sit!* It sounded just like when the scientists opened a bottle of fizzy water. But otherwise, it was quiet. Rat did not like the sound. However, she appreciated it. It reminded her—stay alert.

Rat had worked hard for three days,

44

sneaking back and forth from the food machines on Ring 9 to her nest on Ring 5. What a long trip! Rat did not like the lightness as the fake gravity weakened. The weaker gravity was about the only thing she did not like about her nest. It made her feel less connected to the space station, less able to escape danger. So on each trip for food, Rat practiced. She practiced running and climbing and dodging until she could move as easily anywhere on the space station as she did on Earth.

One nice thing—the food got lighter as she carried it *in*. Rat looked at the packages of food piled around her like a fortress wall. Up close to her bed lay her special prize: three rolls of liverwurst.

Silly boy, not liking liverwurst.

Rat stopped writing to the boy once she got what she wanted. She concentrated on food gathering. Now Rat wondered: What did his last e-mail say? She missed knowing. She liked the way the boy talked to her.

Not like the scientists: They just ordered Rat to do things. The boy was different. He wanted something from Rat, too. It was not the same thing the scientists wanted. She did not understand exactly what it was. She guessed, though, that SORRY, NO MAIL would make him unhappy.

Rat smoothed the last tangled bit of her lavender coat just right. She looked at her supplies. They would keep her fat for a long time! That made her very happy. The boy should be happy, too.

Rat went quickly through small air shafts. They were cozy and quiet. Her whiskers touched the sides. Then she came to the central air shaft. It was like a gigantic toilet-paper tube. It went from all the way *out* to all the way *in*. Lightbulbs set in rows blurred into a fuzzy glow far from Rat. The walls were covered with pipes and wires. Some pipes crisscrossed from one side to the other.

Rat paused to gather her nerve. She did not like crossing to the other side. Of course, she had crossed it dozens of times already—and it was much easier without holding on to a liverwurst. Still, crossing was scary. *Out* ended in a big fan that blew air into the vents. A grate covered the blades, to protect humans, not rats. If Rat fell, she would go right through the grate. Then *chop-chop-chop* . . .

Rat shivered from nerves and cold. The wind made it too cold to stand there hesitating. With careful steps, she climbed out onto the nearest pipe. The air rushed and roared. It blew her fur all the wrong way. That annoyed Rat. She walked as fast as she dared. Her tail bobbed, just touching the surface of the pipe, ready to wrap around it quick if she slipped. In the middle of the central shaft, the thin pipe connected to a big fat one. This pipe was so big, it was practically flat for a rat. Rat scurried on the broad metal curve of the pipe, confident. Soon she was moving through a quiet and cozy air shaft again.

Rat heard voices. They echoed along the shaft connected to the recreation room. It must be family time. Rat went to see.

Nanny, the boy, and his parents were there. The mother was saying, "No bad behavior? What's gotten into you? I mean, how nice! Isn't it nice, Greg?"

"Ummm . . . I guess. I'm still annoyed about this, though," the father said. He shook the plastic bag he was holding. The shredded bits of paper inside flashed yellow. They looked like kernels of corn.

"I *said* I was sorry." The boy crossed his arms.

"Nanny is concerned," said Nanny. "The boy is spending sixty-two point three percent of his time in his room. Nanny cannot go into his room. Nanny does not know what the boy is doing."

The boy said, "I'm e-mailing. I've got a pen pal."

"Oh darling, that *is* nice," said the

mother. She glanced at her watch. "What a relief you've found something to occupy you just now. There's less than twenty-four hours until solar maximum."

The father said, "It's so exciting, Jeff. You should come to the lab and see. We're about to look into the heart of the sun!"

The boy flushed red. "Don't you want to know about my pen pal?"

"The boy cannot have a pen pal," Nanny said. "I monitor all communications. The boy has received no e-mail messages in the past six days."

"I have, too!" The boy stomped his foot. "Nanny is lying!"

"My report is accurate. I have records—"

The mother fluttered her hands in front of Nanny's glowing green eye. "Oh, no, no more paper!"

"I have the e-mail! Come see! Come on!"

The father looked at his watch. "We don't have time for—"

"Nanny's wrong wrong wrong!" the boy

shouted. "Come see! Your stupid Sun will last a billion years!"

"Jeff, I won't have—" the mother began to say.

The loudspeaker on the wall filled the room with the captain's voice. "Attention! All science personnel. Attention! Report immediately to the cafeteria. And bring that boy!"

Nanny's glowing eye swiveled to look at the boy. The parents looked at the boy. The boy bit his lip. They all left the room.

Rat followed them by her secret ways. The closer she got to the cafeteria, the stronger the smell of human became. There were no nice food smells. The sound of many boots moving and a steady beat of words surrounded Rat. *Grumble-grumble-grumble.* The scientists were bothered. They were busy and important and annoyed by the interruption.

Rat peeked out of an air vent.

About twenty scientists were squashed

into the room. Rat saw only the backs of their heads because they were looking at the captain. He stood in front of the food machines, scowling. His dark, squinty gaze roamed the room.

Quickly Rat ducked back into the shadows. She did not like those eyes! The fur at the back of her head prickled. She smoothed it down with two swipes of a paw.

The captain said, "We have a thief."

What a surprise! The scientists quieted.

"What's been stolen?"

"Food," said the captain. *Thump!* He smacked the front of one of the machines. "The fabricators say more has gone out than the waste machines have collected."

Rat startled straight up on her back legs at this news. She rubbed her front paws all over her face as if waking up from a bad dream. The machines count poop? How could Rat have known that? Wicked wicked machines!

"What kind of food?"

The captain read from a list: "Peanut butter, smooth. Oaty oats cereal. Swiss cheese. Peanut butter cookies. Some butter. Three rolls of liverwurst."

Rat had made a mistake. She should have taken only little bits at a time. Too late now. Rat's teeth gnashed together. She sank them into the soft black coating on a wire so that no one would hear them.

Maybe they would blame the boy. They always blamed the boy!

Rat peeked again. Heads turned this way. Heads turned that way. Then all the heads turned toward the door where the boy stood with Nanny and his parents.

"I don't even *like* liverwurst," the boy shouted. "Tell them, Mom. I *never* eat liverwurst!"

"I think so . . . ," said the mother. "Nanny?"

"Mom!" the boy said.

"He is a naughty boy," Nanny said. "He never eats his liverwurst."

Rat did not care if they laughed at the boy. She was worried what might happen if they did not blame him for the missing food. She was not paying attention to what her teeth were doing. They bit the wire too deep.

Flash!

Rat's back arched.

Snap!

Rat saw her tail crack like a whip and a ball of electricity blaze off the tip, before the shock knocked her out.

Chapter Six

The Hunters

The lights went out with a loud pop.

Everyone feared the worst: meteor hit—*decompression*!

Jeff sucked in a desperate lungful of air. Held it.

The green glow from Nanny's eye revealed open mouths, wide eyes, hands at chests, and couples reaching for each other. Everyone was afraid. Everyone imagined: My next breath is death. We will freeze and shatter like lightbulbs dropped on a hard floor.

The stale breath burned deep inside Jeff.

Dad's arm came around his chest and pulled him into a protective hug that squashed the air out. Jeff struggled, but then he had to breathe. . . .

And there was air.

And the emergency lights came on.

There was no hole in the wall, no sound of air rushing out into space, no disaster. Jeff slumped into Dad's warmth pressing all along his back. Mom pressed close, too. Jeff's arm brushed her arm. Mom gave his hand a tense squeeze.

"Relax everyone," the captain said. "Probably just a blown fuse."

"Hey! There's smoke!"

White smoke floated out of an air vent.

"Emergency! Emergency!" Nanny pushed people aside with its padded gripper arms. The right arm telescoped up. Foam squirted from the end into the vent. The smoke stopped.

"I've got a screwdriver," Dad said. One more tightening of his hug, then Dad headed for the vent. Jeff followed. Mom and the others crowded behind them. The rip of so many boots at once sounded like ocean waves coming fast against the shore.

Jeff got pressed against the captain. He tried not to mind the squashy warmth.

Dad pulled a chair under the vent, stepped onto it, pried the grate off, and handed it down to Jeff. It was slick with foam that smelled of ozone and smoke. Dad scooped handfuls out of the vent.

Dad stood on his tiptoes and said, "I can't see much."

He put his arm in and fumbled around.

"Wait. I've got something."

Dad drew out something long and thin. It was a broken wire. "It's been chewed!"

One of the biologists examined it. "These marks are from rodent dentition. From the size, I guess rat."

"Let me see that!" demanded the captain. Jeff saw, too. Dozens of teeth marks scored the black covering of the wire. The marks came in neat pairs. "Who's using rats?"

"Nobody is," the biologist said.

That set off a storm of speculation. How did a rat get here? Where did it come from? How was it surviving? Was it a normal rat, or a Modified?

The biologist jumped on that suggestion. "Oh I hope not, they can be the devil to catch!"

"I don't care what it is or how it got here," the captain said. "I just want it dead before it chews something important. Get the chief engineer here immediately!"

Nanny said, "Nanny will be restored to original form?"

"Yes," said the captain. "Then Nanny will get that rat!"

"Good," said Nanny, and the green eye brightened.

Jeff's skin went all tingly. What was going to happen?

The chief engineer arrived, carrying a toolbox. The captain gestured at Nanny and said, "Get rid of that pink stuff. I want my prowler back, *now*!"

A prowler? Nanny? Jeff always thought Nanny had been thrown together from spare parts—just a hasty job to deal with an unexpected problem: him.

The chief engineer grabbed the rim of Nanny's Frisbee-shaped head and pulled it off. Someone gasped.

"Don't worry. It's got its own power supply." The engineer set Nanny's head on the table, then went to work on the pink foam. Underneath were thin, shiny metal tubes with knobby parts connected by cables.

Jeff watched the green eye watch the chief engineer strip the padding off the grippers. Now Jeff understood: They had turned a ninja robot into a *baby-sitter.* No wonder Nanny hated him!

The grippers snapped off just like pulling a plug out of a socket. With the captain's help, the chief engineer lifted the barrel-shaped part up and away. Hidden inside was a smaller, shiny black body only as tall as Jeff's knees. It was shaped like a motorcycle helmet, the kind with a mirror visor, so you can't see inside. But Jeff saw through the opening on top. Inside were wheels and motors and batteries and wires and other things he didn't recognize.

The captain was in such a hurry that he dropped Nanny's head trying to pop it into place. It clattered and stuck crooked-ways in the opening of the body. An annoyed smack seated it properly.

The grippers were plugged in. With a buzz they shrank and disappeared into the shiny black casing. Now Nanny looked like a super-fancy vacuum cleaner without the hose, but Nanny was a prowler. Prowlers fought like soldiers. They made repairs, inside or out in space. They were very expensive, and there was only one, even on a big space station like this.

"Get back, everyone. Move those tables away," the chief engineer said. Another wave of boot-ripping tore the air. "Systems check. Go."

For a few seconds Nanny stood ticking quietly. Then Nanny moved, and everyone jumped. Nanny went sideways, backward, forward, then sideways again. Nanny's head spun all the way around while the bottom stayed still. The bottom spun around while the top stayed still. Then bottom and top both spun, but in opposite directions.

Nanny circled the room, asking, "Target? Target?"

Blasters poked out. They blew holes in the discarded barrel-shaped section. Grippers grabbed it. Twisted it. Slicers sliced it. Stabbers punched holes in it. Nanny tossed it against the wall. Nanny stopped, sleek and quietly ticking once again.

"Wow!" Jeff said. The air smelled burned. The taste of vaporized metal coated his tongue.

Nanny said, "I am ready for the hunt."

"But Nanny's too big!" Jeff said.

"Hush, Jeff," Mom said.

"It's true. Nanny won't fit in the vent."

Slowly the green eye turned to stare at Jeff. Nanny said, "Ignorant boy, you never study your lessons."

"Ha-ha-ha." The captain laughed, then said to Nanny, "Show him!"

Rattles, bumps, and pings sounded inside Nanny. A little robot dropped out of a hatch at the front. It was no bigger than a mouse, except for the jaws. It looked like false teeth on wheels—alligator teeth. Two tubes waved behind the jaws. Two antennae with glittery eyes bobbed behind the tubes. The little robot skittered around the room, then snapped at Jeff's toes.

"Get away!" Jeff cried, nearly falling as he yanked his too-loose boots backward. Mom and Dad stepped back from the ferocious little robot, too.

"Don't worry. It won't eat *you!*" The captain picked it up. He put it in his palm and held it toward Jeff. The jaws chattered, *snap-snap-snap*. Between snaps Jeff could hear the tubes sucking air.

"This is a little bit of Nanny that can go almost anywhere. We call it a sniffer. For the next few hours or so, you'll be seeing quite a few of these around," the captain said. He put it into the vent. It disappeared, nearly silent on its tiny rubber wheels.

"Tracking," said Nanny.

Would it find the rat right away? If it did, would it bring the rat back alive or dead? Would it bring it back at all? Jeff stared at the vent, waiting, just like everyone else. As the waiting stretched into minutes, some of the scientists got nervous. They wondered, What if the rat is not caught? What if it chews something important?

Mom asked, "Could it damage our equipment, Greg?"

All Mom cared about was her work. Usually that would have annoyed Jeff. But right now he found himself curiously calm and alert. He felt the nudge of an idea. If the sniffer failed . . .

"Report," Nanny said. Jeff held his breath. "The sniffer cannot find the animal. There are many trails in many air shafts. Either one rat has been on station for a long time or there are many rats. I must go hunting."

"Many rats! Many!" the captain snapped. "I won't have it! Get to work, top priority."

"Captain, sir?" Jeff said.

"What?!" The captain glared at him.

Mom touched his shoulder, squeezed.

Jeff ignored Mom's warning. Jeff ignored the quick snap of Nanny's head in his direction. "Sir, remember . . . you promised . . . wouldn't this? I mean, I want to hunt—"

Nanny chirped, "I need no help."

"Quiet, Nanny. I did promise, didn't I? And then I forgot, didn't I?" The captain rubbed his chin for a moment, his whiskers rasping in the quiet room. "Hmmm. Why not? Yes, yes you can."

"Will it be dangerous?" Dad asked.

The captain smiled, and Jeff felt his own mouth trying to smile in the same sinister way.

"Only for the rat!"

Chapter Seven

Narrow Escape

The horrible foam got into Rat's nose. It woke her up. Lucky for Rat. Even though it stuck to her whiskers and fur. Even though it stank of chemicals and made her tongue feel numb when she groomed it off. Without the foam in her nose, the fingers might have got her. Instead, when the fingers touched her, Rat was awake, and she ran.

Rat fled to her nest. Panic allowed no other choice. As soon as her paws touched the shredded-paper bedding, the panic disappeared from her legs like air out of a balloon. Rat collapsed on her bed, panting.

Dumb dumb dumb! If only she hadn't taken so much food at once. If only she hadn't bitten so deep. If only she'd studied more of the lesson. If only . . .

With each new thought Rat felt dumber and dumber until she felt completely stupid. Not only that—her tail hurt, and she smelled bad.

Do something!

She found a packet of butter. *Nip-nip-nip.* She sliced it open. It hurt to nibble! Her teeth felt loose in their sockets.

Rat scooped some butter onto her left paw. She twitched her tail around and caught it with her right paw. She looked at the puffy blister.

At least the spark didn't blind her.

Gently. Gently. Rat spread the soothing butter over the blister. She ground her teeth against the pain.

At least the electricity didn't kill her.

She was a lucky rat, even if she did make a mistake.

Pffssss-ssit!

Rat flashed into a shadowy hollow place, upsetting half her supplies with her powerful kick. It was only the mysterious noise, but Rat's nerves did not know that. Not until she sniffed. Not until she listened. Too much thinking, and the mind got in the way.

Rat took a deep breath. She groomed her whiskers slowly. She had made a game of the gentle noise surprising her. Not now. Now she did not want any surprises. The fingers had been a terrible surprise. Rat had never expected to feel human touch again. Then the fingers came, so strangely pink without the horrible-smelling gloves on them. Rat knew the feel of human skin from when her tail sometimes touched a scientist's arm. But bare fingers on her fur—never!

And never again! Rat rubbed fiercely at the spot beside her nose where the fingers had touched.

Rat paused. The fingers did not get her. Did they find the wire?

If they did, Rat might be only between dangers.

Think! If they found the wire, what would they do?

At the laboratory the scientists used terrible robots for catching animals that escaped. A place with gobblers and Nanny and so many other busy, scurrying robots would have sniffers. Rat could hide from people. They were big and clumsy. Their senses were dull. Sniffers were harder. They almost ruined her escape from the scientists. Small, fast, and vicious, sniffers tracked your smell. And oh how Rat stank! They would find her in a second!

Rat washed her coat. She washed with a fury. The chemical made her feel sick, but she must get clean or—Rat stopped in midlick. Her tongue poked between her teeth. She didn't smell like a rat, did she?

No more washing. She would stink instead. Sniffers did not hunt fire foam. Clever Rat!

Rat looked left. Rat looked right. She crept back to her nest. With quick sweeps of her paws, she pulled the scattered bedding into a comfortable pile. Rat listened once more, then curled up in a tight ball, careful not to lie on her tail. She would not be safe in her nest for long. Too many of her tracks led here. She must leave soon. She had been hungry and lonely before. Now she would be hungry and lonely and hunted. Though Rat did not shed tears, deep down in her heart, she cried.

Where could she go? Where would she be safe from robots? Where would she find food?

Rat looked at the food she had worked so hard for. It must be left behind. But there was one way to take some with her. Rat sliced through the plastic with her teeth. She pressed her nose into the squishy, meaty goodness. The soft food didn't bother her teeth, and it soothed her belly.

Good. Good.

Maybe she was wrong. Maybe they just sent a fix-it and never found the wire.

Rat shuddered. She could not forget the fingers.

How could she find out for sure?

The boy would know.

Yes, the boy. Rat remembered the tiny gobbler that never came after the cookie crumbs in the room. Nanny never entered the room. Only the messy boy. She could hide there. She would get food.

Rat listened at all the paths from her nest.

Nothing sneaking.

She set off.

Chapter Eight

Hunting

I will not complain, Jeff repeated to himself as he followed Nanny down the empty corridor. But the back of his right heel hurt where the gripper boot rubbed. He was hungry and tired. The strap of the gun dug into his shoulder. I must not complain.

Where were they? Jeff didn't know. Nanny did. Jeff dared not bother Nanny with a question like that. Maybe Ring 3—or was that the last one? Somewhere far *in,* anyway. The tight curve in the floor told Jeff that. Not very far ahead of them the floor seemed to curl up into the ceiling. At least the gravity was weaker this far *in.* The gun felt less heavy. But he still had to pull hard to make the boots let go of the sticky carpet strip. That made his heel smart.

Hours ago the captain had handed him the gun. The gun made his parents nervous. They almost wouldn't let him go. But the captain told them it was a SmartGun. He quickly punched several buttons on it before handing it to Jeff.

"There now, perfectly safe, even for a boy!" The captain laughed. "Can't have people blowing holes in the walls, you know!"

Mom said, "I guess it's okay." And Dad nodded.

Then the captain sent Jeff on his way with this advice: "Stick with Nanny, boy, and everything will be fine."

Jeff obeyed, creeping and sneaking behind Nanny through the stale-smelling and silent parts of the space station. When Nanny moved, Jeff moved. His boots made a soft *scritch-rip, scritch-rip* sound. Nanny's motor buzzed. When Nanny stopped, Jeff stopped. When Nanny looked around with the one green eye, Jeff held his breath. He strained his eyes and ears into the gloomy bigness, alert to any hint of a rat. It was fun at first. But they had been doing this since the meeting in the cafeteria. That had been just after lunch. Jeff was sure they had prowled right through supper time by now. *In* and *out* and around and around, and nothing happened.

Another jab of pain. He clenched his teeth. Once again he blamed Mom for forgetting, imagining the boots side by side in the front hall, in plain sight. Good for nothing on Earth.

He bet the blister was huge, the kind that pops and bleeds and gets infected. They would have to cut his foot off. It happened to prisoners on long marches, Jeff knew. And this was a long march! Jeff had never walked so much in his whole life— not even at camp. Maybe they would notice when he lost a foot trying to save the project from some dumb—

"Ow!"

Jeff smacked his knee against Nanny's hard shell. He hadn't noticed that the robot had stopped. After making an angry, sizzly sound like a hive of disturbed bees, Nanny went quiet.

The silence made Jeff's ears throb. No machines hummed. No air fans whispered. The corridor was so dark the colors on the piping didn't show. Only one tiny bulb glowed yards away. It lit up a closed hatch with a sign saying DANGER—OFF-LIMITS. Another abandoned part of the space station. No reason to search there; even a rat needed air.

But Nanny did not turn back.

What was up?

Jeff forced his eyes open as wide as they could go. His finger curled over the cold, hard trigger. How dangerous the gun felt! The automatic targeting beam came on. It cast a dinner-plate-sized circle of light as bright as sunshine. Briefly the light blazed off Nanny's laser-proof armor, dazzling

Jeff's dark-adjusted eyes. Then Jeff aimed into the shadowy places.

Come on, rat!

But he could barely see, so he hoped the rat would wait a minute before showing up. Nanny was not bothered by the sudden change from dark to light. Nanny had sensors for heat and motion. Jeff despaired, not for the first time since the hunt began: How would he ever get the rat first?

Something clattered as loud as spilled pennies just above his head. Eyes-hand-gun all jerked toward the sound. Jeff almost pulled the trigger, but it was just a sniffer in the air vent. Its jagged teeth glittered like a mouthful of braces in the targeting beam. The wormy eye tubes bobbed.

Jeff let out a whoosh of breath. He slumped against the wall, then slowly sank to the deck. While Nanny talked to the sniffer, he pulled off his boot. The sock came next. Sure enough, a blister as big as his thumb—puffy and white with red all around it. It was shaped like a lima bean, Jeff's least favorite food after liverwurst.

Nanny reported, "There is a pattern to the trails. The sniffers need more time."

"Can we rest then? I'm starving!" Jeff took off his pack.

"Nanny needs no food. Nanny needs no rest. Nanny does not get blisters."

"So what? You still can't find it, can you? Even with all those sniffers! Maybe I'd have better luck without you!"

"Let's find out," Nanny said, and zipped up the corridor.

"Hey! Stop! Come back!"

Nanny did not take orders from Jeff. It raced beyond the point where the floor and ceiling appeared to pinch together.

Jeff rolled to his feet, or meant to. But he pushed too hard and lifted into the air. He corkscrewed twice before he caught the floor with the toe of his booted foot. Con-nected at last, he ran—*scritch-rip-thump, scritch-rip-thump*. Running with one bare foot in this weak gravity tested all his skill. Every pump of his leg tried to carry him into the ceiling. He struggled and wobbled and began to feel sick to his stomach. He stopped, hands on knees, puffing. Many passages led *in* and *out* here. Nanny could have taken any one. He held his breath, listened. No motor noise. He would never find Nanny.

Who cares? He didn't want Nanny, anyway. He wanted the rat!

Scritch-rip-thump, scritch-rip-thump. Slowly Jeff walked back to where he'd left all his things. Food first, then a bandage for the blister, then . . .

Jeff tried to think what to do next. But he had no idea how to hunt for a rat. His only chance was to be with Nanny and shoot first.

Without him Nanny moved faster, Nanny moved quieter. Nanny would get the rat. He had ruined his one chance.

CHAPTER NINE

Bad News

Rat made a nest in the boy's laundry drawer. She shaped a red T-shirt into a bowl just right for her to curl up in. The boy smelled nice. That surprised Rat. Scientists stank of sharp chemicals, horrible choking perfumes, and rubber gloves. Rat pushed her nose deep into the fabric. The surprise nice smell comforted her. Rat might need the boy's help if they were hunting her. She was glad he didn't stink.

Rat worried when she first dropped into the boy's room. There were not many places to hide on a space station. It was so shipshape, with cubbyholes, cabinets, and closets. A place for everything, and everything in its place—even in the boy's room, though he was messy. Usually a drawer would not be a good place to hide. But the laundry drawer under the bed had a vent in back that drew away the smell of old clothes. Rat used the computer maps to find out how the vent above the bed connected to the one in the laundry drawer. She got in through the vent, and could escape that way if she needed to. The drawer had a screen on front. Rat could see out while safely hidden in the shadows.

Safe at last. The fire foam had protected her, though its scent was going away now. Rat just smelled like herself. She liked that. Life was too strange lately, with too many strange new things.

She curled into a ball and pulled her tail around under her nose. That hurt. Rat studied the ugly red blister covered with messy butter. At least it was healing.

What a mistake she had made. But so what? She was new at this—new at being free.

Rat took a deep breath. She was a rat

who lived by her wits. She had gotten the boy to study the food machines. She would get him to help her now. All the muscles under her lavender-colored coat relaxed. Her body was falling asleep, but her mind was not ready. In this safe place her mind wanted to take time to understand.

If it weren't for her wits, Rat might still be at the lab. Comfortable. Or maybe dead. In the lab there was always food and water. The temperature was always the same. The scientists taught her sign language, computers, and many other things. But they never taught her about the world outside, or why she was different from the other rats, or who her mother had been.

And they were evil. One day her neighbor would make perfect sense—for an ordinary rat. Then he would come back from where the scientist took him. He ate and drank and moved around, but he no longer sniffed noses through the bars or talked to Rat. Then one day the cage would be empty, too. This had happened many times. Rat was smart enough to know it might happen to her. But she had not thought about escaping until she saw the television and, later, the window.

A new lab worker had come. He fed her bits of his liverwurst sandwiches. He always brought a small TV set. He had put the TV on the counter near Rat's cage while he worked. Rat remembered the first program: a documentary on wheat farming in Iowa. There were miles and miles of wheat the same color as the cardboard they put in the cage for her to chew. After the harvest there were miles and miles of *dirt*! What a revelation! Places without walls! Places almost without people!

The weather reports had fascinated Rat. So many new words: cloudy, hot, cold, rain, snow, wind, clear skies, breezy . . .

What were these mysterious things? Rat did not know. Until the window.

The scientist had been in a hurry that

day, something forgotten. He had carried Rat into a kind of room she had never been in before: an office. The light inside was yellow, not white like from the tubes in the ceiling. Its brilliance blinded Rat. The cage thunked down. Smells exploded in her nose. She had no idea what these smells were—something like the vegetables they gave her to eat, only more green, more alive. Something like her cage when the shavings hadn't been changed, only sweeter, crumblier, cleaner.

When Rat was able to open her eyes, she thought her cage rested in front of a huge TV. She could see trees, grass, and flower beds with black dirt all bathed in a light so brilliant and clear. The clarity made her feel as if her eyes had never seen before. She could see every leaf that fluttered on the trees. They winked silver-green.

The light darkened, then returned. Rat looked up into the sky—out there was what the TV weatherman had described that morning:

"And now my forecast for today. High pressure will dominate our region, while a cold front moving in from the north will bring partly cloudy skies and a southwesterly breeze by afternoon. . . ."

Rat shook the stupid voice out of her head. It was all so much more beautiful than those words!

Layer upon layer of odors flowed through the open window. Rat stood perfectly still. Her nose worked delicately, sorting, mystified. The scientist fumed, slamming drawers and cursing. Between his noises, Rat heard a new sound. It sounded· like grain pouring into her food bowl, only much softer. This delicious sound came from the leaves of the trees.

The startling light had gradually moved into Rat's cage, yellow as crisp new shavings. She stepped into it. Warmth embraced her. Every hair in her coat glittered. Sunlight. From outside. Wildness, anger, and resolve seized Rat. She began to plan her escape.

And now look at her! Trapped on a space station! It made her want to chew wire, chew lots of wire, chew *all* the wires!

The door opened, and the boy's complaining voice drove everything from Rat's mind. "It wasn't fair! You left me alone for *hours*! Then sneaking up. You *scared* me!"

"Noisy, dull boy," said Nanny. "Lucky *we* are the hunters. Lucky *you* are not a rat. Sleep now."

"I don't want to!"

We?! Rat could not see them. Rat did not let a single muscle even feel a wish to see them. *We are the hunters!*

"Annoying boy, you must."

"You, too, then. You sleep, and we'll start again together."

"Nanny does not sleep."

"Well, go fix something. Just don't hunt anymore. Not until I can help again."

"Nanny does not need help."

"Stop saying that! I'm helping *them,* not you. That's why it's important."

"Them?"

"Mom and Dad. The captain. Don't you remember? The captain said the rat had to be caught quickly before it chewed something important, maybe something that could ruin Mom and Dad's work. That's when they really got excited about my going. So I'm helping them."

How could Rat have been so stupid, thinking the boy was her friend? He was human. Of course he would help them, not her.

"Nanny is not programmed to understand. We are wasting time. Go to sleep." Nanny's motor hummed.

"All right already. I know I have to sleep. But I don't need lots. Come get me in four hours, okay? I'll set my alarm."

"Nanny will work very fast while you sleep. You will not go hunting again."

"Oh yeah? You didn't get it last time you were alone. I don't think you'll get it now."

Nanny clicked. "You are a stubborn boy. Nanny will return in six hours."

"But—"

The door closed.

The boy clomped toward the bed. Besides the *scritch* of his boots, Rat heard a dragging, then a heavy thud as the boy dropped something on the floor. He flopped onto the bed. Rat nudged an eye out of the folds of the T-shirt. She stared at the gun. It looked nearly as big as the boy.

The gun changed everything.

The boy got off the bed. The computer started up, followed by typing. Rat guessed he was writing his pen pal. Telling all about the hunt. Stupid boy! You're trying to *kill* your pen pal.

But the boy did not know that. Rat had to be fair to him.

What would he do if he knew?

The boy shut off the computer. He took something out of a locker. He came back and sat on the bed. He pulled off his boots. Blood stained the back of his right sock. Rat leaned closer to the screen. The sock and then a bloody bandage came off. The broken blister looked more painful than the one on her tail.

The boy set the first-aid kit on the floor. He began to clean his hurt foot. He took sharp, short breaths as he worked. Rat's own tail began to throb as she remembered how much it hurt to touch. The boy gingerly rubbed on ointment. It looked and smelled as if it would work much better than butter. He put on a bandage, working with careful fingers. Rat never saw the boy do anything so neatly before.

The boy put the first-aid kit away, set his alarm clock, then fell into bed still wearing his clothes.

"Please don't let Nanny find it . . . please."

The boy whispered this a few times, then his breathing changed to the rhythms of sleep.

Rat was not so lucky. She slept badly, waking often. She must get the message perfectly right. She dreamed she forgot how to type. Or suddenly, she floated, too light to press the keys. Once the screen filled with paw prints instead of letters.

Each time Rat woke, the bulky shadow of the gun greeted her tired eyes. A flashing light on its control panel winked rapidly, as if excited, as if to say to her, "I know you are there."

Chapter Ten

The Rat

When the alarm rang, Jeff got straight out of bed. He was ready for something to happen. He was ready to make something happen. He grabbed the gun. Lunge. Pivot. Aim.

"Blam-blam-blam!" He yelled these words even though the modern gun did not make such crude noises. It was more fun than quietly saying, *"Zizz-zizz."*

"I got the moves."

Lunge. Hop into reverse crouch. *Thwack!* The blistered heel slammed against the laundry drawer.

"Ow!"

He dropped the gun and fell onto the bed. He rocked back and forth, clutching just above his ankle, trying to throttle the pain. When the throbbing lessened he looked at the clock. Ten more minutes. Would Nanny come? Had there been any real shooting while he was asleep?

Just be ready, Jeff told himself. Don't give Nanny any excuse to leave you behind.

He packed his backpack. He ate a concentrated breakfast ration. He checked the bandage and put on his boots. He brushed his teeth.

Five minutes.

He wanted to check his e-mail. As soon as he turned on the computer, a warning notice flashed on the screen: METEOR RISK HIGH NEXT FOUR HOURS. ALL PERSONNEL TAKE PRECAUTIONS.

That meant lots of jiggles on the space station, maybe even a puncture. Mom and Dad would be nervous wrecks today. Jeff reached into a cubby next to the desk and took out the emergency air mask. He set it next to the keyboard. For once Jeff was glad he'd be with Nanny. He hadn't believed the robot before when it told him it could fix any meteor damage. Now he knew better—the safest place to be in a meteor storm was with a prowler.

He checked his e-mail. SORRY, NO MAIL.

What had happened to his pen pal? The last message said he was sick and not to worry. But Jeff did worry. It made him sad to think he might lose his new friend just like that. What fun if they were *both* hunting the rat—so much more fun than hunting with Nanny! Fat chance his pen pal could ever visit the space station, but it was fun to imagine. Would they meet when he got back to Earth? That might be—

The door buzzed. Jeff spun the chair around and hurled himself out of it. Then he stopped. Was Nanny waiting there with a dead rat dangling from a gripper?

The door opened and there was Nanny. Just Nanny. "Follow me. You are wasting time."

Nanny turned and moved down the corridor. Jeff grabbed his backpack and gun, and followed. When he caught up, Nanny said, "Progress report: Analysis indicates the rat's nest is in the Mid-Ring workshop. We will find it now. The hunt will end."

"What's the Mid-Ring workshop?"

"The parts for the last five rings were made there. The machines are worn out. The workshop has not been used for twenty years, four months, three days. The records say there is no air in it." Nanny stopped abruptly. Jeff bumped into it. The green eye swiveled to face him. "Sloppy people! The records are wrong! There is air. How can Nanny search properly if the records are wrong?"

Jeff shrugged.

Nanny's eye glowed brighter.

"Sloppy boy," Nanny said. "Where is your emergency mask?"

Jeff touched his belt clip. "Shoot! Left it on the desk. I'd better go get it."

"Delay delay—unacceptable. Top priority: Kill the rat," Nanny droned, and started to move away from Jeff. Then Nanny hesitated, stopped. "Nanny must protect the boy from harm—orders."

Nanny was his protector? He'd thought they'd made the robot just to keep him out of their way.

Nanny spun around. "Go back. Quick."

Jeff hurried. He didn't want Nanny to march him back. What a surprise to see Nanny confused! A perfect example of fuzzy logic. He was telling himself to remember it for Mr. DiSalvo's artificial intelligence class, when he opened the door. The *clickity-tap* of keys immediately drew his attention to the computer. Something lavender stood on the keyboard.

"Hey!"

It startled, turning eyes as black as sunspots on him.

Jeff had never seen a rat before. He didn't know they could be that color. He didn't know rats had eyes like that, or such big, pink ears. He wasn't even sure rats had ears. They were so delicate. The light from the monitor shone through them. They had dark little veins, just like a leaf.

"Alert! Alert! Privacy override!"

Jeff's legs went out from under him. The world tilted, like a bad step while running.

Meteor!

But then he felt Nanny's hard shell shoving against the side of his leg, collapsing his knee. He flailed for balance. His boots slid on Nanny's smoothness. Door frame. Grab it. He missed and toppled down on Nanny. Motors whined shrilly. Flashes of laser fire lit the room. *Zizz. Zizz.* The wall above his bed exploded in a shower of hot sparks.

Nanny regained its wheels and rushed to the bed, grippers extending as it moved. It ripped the grating off the vent. Something fell onto the bed, bounced, rolled off.

The rat? But it couldn't be, because Nanny paid no attention to it. Nanny seized the edge of the vent and hauled its body up so that its eye could see inside. *Zizz-zizz. Zizz-zizz.*

Nanny dropped onto the bed. *Rattle-bump-ping:* A sniffer popped out, jaws snapping madly. Nanny lifted it into the vent, then somersaulted to the floor.

"Get out of the way," Nanny said.

"*That* was the rat! What was it doing here?" Jeff asked, scrambling to his feet.

"Get out of the way," Nanny said.

"Where are you going?"

"It is ninety percent likely the animal will flee to its nest. I will be there."

Jeff picked up his gun. "Me too!"

"*No.* You will stay here."

"That's not fair! I would have blasted

it. It's just . . . well, I thought rats were brown!"

"You are an ignorant boy. Move aside."

"No!"

"Yes!" Nanny seemed to get bigger, like a porcupine raising its quills. Dozens of mechanical arms poked out of hidden holes in Nanny's black armor and waved and clattered. Nanny lurched forward.

Jeff meant to hold his ground, but the instant before Nanny touched him, he flinched and let Nanny scoot past.

CHAPTER ELEVEN

THE CHASE

Rat was not running as fast as she wanted to. Rat was not running as fast as she needed to.

Faster! Faster!

But the metal air duct was not very grippy. Rat's sharp nails and soft toes slapped and slipped. The sniffer motor whined behind her, louder every moment. The shrill noise hurt her sensitive ears.

Rat ran straight toward her goal. No point in dodging this way or that. Once a sniffer got on your trail, it never lost you. It followed you by sight and scent and heat and many other signs. The only way to escape was to break the trail completely. There was only one place Rat might do that: the central air shaft. She needed to leap all the way across it. She must do it before the sniffer saw her.

Such a huge leap!

Rat did not know if she could make it. She would need all her courage. But her heart hurt. Not just from working so hard to feed the burning muscles in her legs. No, it was the green eye pushing past the boy's legs—a sight that seemed to be painted on the back of her eyes. The boy had startled her, but it was the eye so unexpectedly close to the floor that nearly cost Rat her life. Where were the soft pads? The round body? Surprise and confusion had made her hesitate, almost too long.

Hunted by such a terrible machine. And the boy helping it.

The breeze grew stronger. It cooled her and put more speed into her legs. A right-angle corner appeared. Rat did not break her pace. She crashed her body into the wall and kicked out with her back legs. She flew four feet before her paws again touched the metal. A dim square of light shone where this air shaft entered the central shaft. And dark beyond it, the square of the opposite air shaft. Her target. It looked no bigger than a postage stamp.

The breeze grew stronger still. It became an enemy, pushing against her. Would it slow her too much? Her feet slapped. The fan roared. The sniffer motor faded away in her final, desperate sprint.

Something's wrong.

An uneasy feeling came from the part of her brain that knew patterns. Why is that branch shaft there? What is that hole ahead in the floor? Rat realized all her effort had been a waste. She was in the wrong shaft! Having to jump that hole first would break her stride. She could never regain enough speed to make the big leap. It must have happened when she zigzagged to escape the laser blasts. The blinding light, the shower of sparks, the smoke that felt like wood chips up her nose had confused her.

Rat locked her legs, skidded, fell. She tumbled in several bumpy, bouncy, head-over-heels rolls.

She stopped with her nose touching the edge of the hole. Her delicate whiskers brushed the creases of metal, the tiny bumps of rivets. Her brain instantly showed where the hole went, where it came out. This wasn't a disaster after all. Seeing how the hole fit in the maze of air shafts, Rat thought of a plan. She hunched at the edge and drew in a big, confident breath: *The prey was about to become the hunter.*

Her plan to destroy the sniffer was as dangerous as trying to jump across the central air shaft. The sniffer must see her. The sniffer must get very close. Any error in timing, any stumble, would be Rat's last mistake.

The sniffer's motor suddenly went silent.

Rat looked over her shoulder to see it paused at the corner; its eyestalks wobbled, searching. The moment it saw Rat, its jaws started chomping. Rat flattened her ears, but the terrible sound snapped in her like bones breaking. The sniffer moved. Rat jumped the hole and scurried to the very edge of the opening into the central shaft. She poked her head into the breeze.

Yes! There, just a body length *out* from the opening, was the small pipe that went back to the hole in the vent.

Rat faced the sniffer. As the pointed steel teeth drew nearer and nearer Rat told herself, It is mindless, and I am clever.

The sniffer slowed for an instant when it sensed the hole, then *sproing,* it was over on her side.

Rat dropped over the edge and vanished into the small pipe. Silent, without breathing. Slinking without sound. Swift as a snake, Rat flowed through the pipe that made a twisty U-turn back into the hole. Rat popped out right behind the sniffer, which was tilted up on two wheels at the brink, leaning its eyestalks into the central shaft. Rat's toes grasped the riveted edge. Her rear paws bunched for an instant, then head tucked, shoulder forward, she lunged.

Smack!

Rat smashed into the sniffer. It flew into the central shaft. A desperate grab at the frame around the opening; a second suspended, then toenails split, broke, and Rat fell, too.

The sniffer tumbled *out,* bouncing and clattering like a tin can as it hit the pipes crisscrossing the shaft.

Rat fell behind it. The breeze grew stronger and stronger.

Leaves.

Rat did not know why she thought of them. But the precious, remembered images from her first look out the window came sharper. Leaves. Leaves tossed by the wind. They fell, but not straight, not fast.

Maybe . . .

Not much time . . .

But Rat had more time than the sniffer.

Whap! The fan blades shattered it into a hundred glittery nuts, bolts, and computer chips.

Against the instinct that had curled her into a ball, Rat threw her paws wide as if to embrace her fate. She made herself broad. She made herself flat.

Rat fluttered—flew!

Almost.

Her right forepaw brushed a thin pipe. Too quick to grab.

Another, bigger, ahead. But out of reach to her right.

Tilt!

Rat actually changed direction!

Tilt!

Whap!

Rat hit the pipe, curled her body tight, wrapped her tail. Pain flared from the blister, and she nearly let go.

Cling! Cling!

She spun around the pipe once, twice. Stopped.

Her shoulder hurt. Her stomach hurt. Her tail hurt.

Rat watched the fan blades spin. What now? What now?

CHAPTER TWELVE

DISCOVERY

Jeff crossed the threshold and stopped. The air stank of charred plastic and paint and the tingle of zapped molecules. He looked at the keyboard.

Lavender. Why did he know the rat's fur was lavender-colored? It bothered him, that word. If only it had been a plain brown rat, then maybe he would have blasted it before Nanny interfered.

Jeff shied at the memory of the hard metal raking against his leg, the loss of balance, falling . . .

Falling.

Something fell when Nanny tore the grate off the vent above the bed. Jeff thought it was the rat, but that was a mistake. He snapped out of his memories to focus alertly on the room. There it was, just beside the bed: a toilet-paper tube. Jeff picked it up.

Heavy.

The weight surprised his fingers, and he almost dropped it. Cautiously he brought it up to his face. He looked in the end. His heart thumped. He looked in the other end.

"Oh, wow!" he said. "Those got me in so much trouble!"

What were the missing lenses doing stuck in a toilet-paper tube with some gum—*his* gum? No one else on the space station chewed gum. Who made the tube? Why did that person hide it in the vent—*his* vent? Did someone want to get him in more trouble? But that didn't make sense. No one would ever look in the vent.

Jeff put the tube to his eye. He saw a tiny dot of hazy light. Backward. He turned it around. He noticed three little notches in the rim of the tube. Ah! To show which side to look in! Clever.

But *who* had been so clever?

Jeff stared at the tube in his palm. The notches reminded him of the teeth marks on the wire. . . .

Jeff brought the tube to his eye. It seemed as if he had jumped straight across the room and put his nose to the wall. He could see the seam in the wall panel and the tiny nicks in the rivets where the riveting tool had marked them. When he tried to look anywhere else, the image blurred. Jeff knew a few things about lenses and telescopes because his parents worked with them. Sometimes he paid attention when they talked. This homemade spyglass had a fixed focus. It was meant to look at one spot.

Jeff got up on the bed. This put his head almost even with the vent. He leaned against the wall. His nose wrinkled. The charred smell was strongest here. He put the tube to his eye again. The computer monitor filled the eyepiece. Perfectly clear, he saw his last e-mail to his pen pal, now in reply mode, and the beginning of a new message:

DO NOT KILL RATTTTTTTTTTTTTTTTTTT>*&%F)

The rat hadn't just been standing on the keyboard, it had been *typing*. And when Jeff walked in, its little paw with the white cuff—yes, he remembered that now—the paw stood on the T key all the while it stared at Jeff.

Nanny was right. There never were any messages from Earth.

Jeff dropped the tube and leaped for the computer. He opened the in-box and swept the subject lines with his finger. There: no picture.

To: Jeff@spotseeker.orbit
From: newfriend@home.earth
Subject: no picture

I cannot send my picture. But I am very beautiful. I have a lavender coat with white cuffs. Here is how it looks.

The square of color removed all doubt:
I've been hunting my pen pal!
Nanny is hunting my pen pal!
Quick! Quick!
Fingers fumbled on the keys. Slower.

QUERY: station maps, index, workshop.

Three dozen references flashed on the screen. Dumb!

QUERY: miding—delete—Mid-Ring Workshop.

A map appeared showing a huge area on Ring 5.

QUERY: main entrance.

The image automatically zoomed to focus on a giant door in section 3, level 2.
Go!

Stop!

Gun. Now go!

Run. *Run!*

Jeff did not care who saw him. No one could stop him. He would run straight through the captain if he got in the way. But the boots still slipped, and the gun thumped hard against his hip. The bandage began to unravel from the strain. Soon that blister would really begin to hurt.

Chapter Thirteen

Emergency!

Rat sniffed. The air *smelled* untouched. Rat licked her forepaws. She rubbed them all over her nose to make it as clean as could be. Rat lay down and inched to the end of the narrow shaft. Carefully she poked her nose into the dim emptiness beyond. Her nostrils flared and quivered. Yes. Yes. The air was the same, stale and still. Safe.

Ever so slowly Rat oozed out of the shaft into the tunnel. Her nest was only a dozen body lengths farther along. The tunnel had room enough for Rat to swish her tail without touching the sides. But it was too small for humans, too small even for Nanny.

But not for sniffers or gobblers or fix-its, Rat reminded herself. Rat paused to listen, to sniff, to stretch her whiskers into the dimness. Rat had chosen well. Not even those little robots had found this place.

The tunnel was inside the walls of a forgotten part of the space station. Rat never went into that huge room, not once she found the tunnel. It was too open, with too few places to hide. The giant gray machines frightened Rat, though they were covered in thick dust. What were they for? Could they suddenly start up? Better to stay away from them.

There was thick dust in the tunnel, too. Nice dust. It sifted between Rat's toes as she crept closer and closer to her nest. She savored the feel of it so soft under her toes. They hurt from all the running on hard metal. She never found dust anywhere else in the space station. It made her feel the tunnel was another world—a world safe for a rat.

The air took on a spicy tang. A few more steps and Rat's whiskers touched the curlicue edges of torn plastic. She licked the liverwurst. Mmmm—still good! But Rat could not eat any, not yet. Her stomach felt like a hard marble, with no space inside. She moved around, touching everything. Her supplies were exactly where she had left them. She sniffed her nest. Rat, the smells told her. Only Rat.

She hugged the warm pipe. The heat seeped into her tired, hurting body.

Pffss-sit!

Rat flinched, and all the achy places started hurting again.

Stupid noise!

These sudden, mysterious sounds used to be a game, but now she did not need a game. She needed silence. Something might come sneaking during the noise. How could she get rid of it?

The noise came from behind a big metal box on the wall opposite her nest. Rat investigated it. Under a tiny blue light, there was a switch turned to ON. There was an OFF, too. So maybe she *could* get rid of it. But what would *that* do? Would something bad happen? Would a fix-it come?

There was a label. In the dim light, Rat had to press her nose against the box to read the letters—one by one. Then she put them together in her head: STABILIZER ROCKET #724 CONTROL BOX.

What did that mean? Rat sat back. She scratched, though she did not have an itch. Something new. Even now, with her life in danger, Rat did not know enough about the space station. It was too easy to make a mistake.

She hated the space station.

Pffss-sit!

That noise again! Rat reached for a wire, teeth bared and ready to rip into the black coating—

Bang!

The cover exploded off the box. Luckily Rat had dipped her head, reaching for the wire, or the cover would have hit her. Spinning, clattering, it tore into her supplies, scattered her nest. Inside the box air hissed out of a hole the diameter of a toilet-paper tube. Dust went up, thick and choking. It gathered into a whirlwind that streamed into the box and swirled out into space like water going down a drain.

The hole wanted Rat, too. Her body lurched toward it. She scrambled to get to the warm pipe. The air was full of dust, cookie crumbs, and shreds of paper from her nest. They battered Rat and tugged her fur every which way. She clung to the pipe, struggling for breath. It was like trying to breathe with your nose pinched tight. Only a little air etched a path into her lungs. The greedy hole wanted it all.

Faintly Rat heard the sound of sirens and words. They echoed through the vents, soft and muffled.

"Emergency! Emergency! Meteor impacts! Decompression! *Emergency!"*

Click-click-click.

Rat barely heard those clicks, faint as the *tap-tap-tap* of the scientists' shoes in the hallway outside the lab. The sucking sound quieted. The dust settled.

Was it over?

Shapes blacker than the dimness began sliding across the tunnel to either side of Rat. The space station was protecting itself by sealing off the tunnel around the leak. The clicks had been the sound of all the shafts nearby shutting tight. Another second, and she would be trapped, she would suffocate. Rat seized the last roll of liverwurst and held it before her like a shield. She kicked off toward the shrinking arch of dimness. Whiskers brushed metal on both sides. She heard a click back near the tip of her tail.

Rat landed on her side and bounced once with the liverwurst. She lay still, panting. She had nearly lost her life.

Her fault? Another mistake? But she never touched the wire, or the switch. As

116

more air got to her brain, Rat remembered the words: *Emergency meteor decompression.* A moment longer, and they made sense. Not her fault.

The tunnel walls seemed too close suddenly. What if more meteors came crashing through? She got up to search for a way out. The liverwurst was heavy, but she could not leave it behind. She did not want to lose everything she had worked so hard for. She did not want to escape decompression only to starve.

An open shaft led out of the tunnel. Rat shoved the liverwurst in. She followed, pushing it along ahead of her. The shaft angled steeply and the liverwurst started to slide. There was too much dust for Rat to get a grip and she slid helplessly behind it. The walls disappeared. A moment in air, then a floor, *thump*—not hard enough to hurt. The liverwurst lay next to her.

Rat felt bigness all around. She was in the forgotten room. It was silent and dark.

The sounds of the emergency couldn't be heard here. Though her lungs burned for air, lots of air, Rat forced herself to breathe in tiny, nearly silent sips.

A door whooshed open, the sound dull and distant. Light blazed a narrow wedge through the center of the room. Not near Rat. She stood absolutely still. She planned where she would run. She might have to leave the liverwurst.

Rrriiippp! A Velcro boot. Rat recognized it.

What was the boy doing here?

Then the sniffer got her.

Chapter Fourteen

The Rescue

Jeff pressed the button over and over. But he could not make the elevator go *in* any faster. He sagged against the wall. There was time to catch his breath; time to think. Only bad thoughts came: What if Nanny . . . What if Mom and Dad . . . What if the rat . . .

The loudspeaker spluttered: *"Emergency! Emergency! Decompression in Ring Eight section D. Nanny, report for damage control. Emergency!"*

Yes. Go away. Go help, Jeff thought. Forget the rat.

Jeff had never felt the space station jiggle so sharply or so often. The meteor hits nearly knocked him off his feet as he ran to the elevator. There must be a big hole somewhere, or more than one. Somebody might even be hurt. But Ring 8, section D wasn't anywhere near where his parents worked. It wasn't near the Mid-Ring workshop, either. Good thing, because he'd forgotten the air mask.

The elevator stopped, and its door snapped open. Jeff looked across an unlit corridor as wide as a street. He gagged with his first breath. The air smelled spoiled. Opposite him the elevator cast a square light on a huge door crisscrossed with bands of steel. The sign read: MID-RING WORKSHOP MAIN ENTRY. Jeff took a step.

Rrriiipppp.

His knee flew up out of control and knocked against his arm. The gun jerked up and hit him on the chin. He stumbled back into the elevator. The clack of his teeth echoed like a cackle in the vastness.

Stupid!

Jeff ran his tongue over his teeth. Nothing broken. No taste of blood. He should have adjusted his step to the gravity here, but worrying about everything else, he'd forgotten. Mid-Ring had half the gravity of Outer Ring, where Jeff spent most of his time.

Nanny didn't make mistakes. What chance did he have to save the rat, making mistakes like that? But then he remembered: Nanny had been called away.

Jeff stepped out of the elevator again. He kept a stiff leg and walked with a shuffle. Sensing the motion, the lights in the corridor turned on, popping and flickering. Half of them didn't work. Dust swirled all around him.

The elevator door closed, leaving Jeff with the silence. No air fans whirled here. No machinery chirped. Even the sound of the emergency sirens didn't reach this place. Jeff shivered. He didn't like it, but it might be just right for a rat, a rat that needed a place to hide.

He shuffled up to the door. It was three

times his height. Steel beams as thick as his waist framed it. Incredibly there was some rust. Because of the air and the robots not knowing . . .

So Nanny was right, people had been sloppy. He reached for the door's OPEN button and hesitated.

Something was wrong.

The silence! No sirens, no announcements. Nanny could not have heard the call. Nanny was still here.

Jeff stabbed the button. The door slid aside, revealing machines, row upon row of them. They spread in all directions, far beyond where the light from the corridor reached. Some were as big as elephants. They cast enormous shadows against the back wall of the workshop.

How would he ever find a rat in there? But there was no time to waste on doubts. He *had* to find it. Jeff hurried over the threshold.

Rrriiippp—SNAP!

The snap sounded like a book being slammed shut.

A scream. Jeff froze in midstride. The scream crescendoed to an agonized shriek that cut off abruptly. He had never heard such a sound in real life, only in horror movies. He felt sick, waiting for more. But the echo faded. The silence came back briefly. Then Jeff heard small sounds he did not understand.

Thump-clatter-scratch-scratch-thump-clatter.

The sounds repeated in a desperate rhythm. Somehow they were more unnerving than the scream had been.

A shrill, mechanical drone overwhelmed them—Nanny's motor. Far, impossibly far away, he saw a green glow sweeping along the back wall. The sounds must be the rat, struggling with a sniffer—*and Nanny was closing in for the kill.*

Jeff ran. In the half-gravity each surging step became a giant's stride. He moved like a gazelle, bounding. He did not have to find a path between the machines—he jumped over the smaller ones. He sprang from top to top of the biggest. The half-gravity worked for him now. He was too slow for Nanny in the Outer Ring, but here he had a chance. Wheels could only turn so fast, no matter how weak the gravity.

Jeff landed on the last machine. An open space as wide as a street stretched to the back wall. The light from the door faded here, leaving a murky twilight. To his left the greenish glow moved with the eye burning brightly at the center of it. No other part of Nanny was visible. He could not see the rat. But he heard the struggle off to his right. A minute, maybe two, and the gap would be closed.

Jeff raised the gun and peered in the scope. The target beam flared. He aimed.

"Nanny, stop!" His voice quivered, feeble. It was swallowed by the room. Sweat slicked his palms. Jeff yelled, "Stop! I'll shoot!"

Stop! Stop! Shoot! Shoot!

The words were loud enough this time, but Nanny paid no attention. Jeff pressed the trigger.

Nothing happened.

He did it again and again.

But each time the scope simply flashed: WRONG TARGET.

Of course! The gun would only shoot rats. That's what the captain was doing when he programmed it. That's why he told his parents hunting would be perfectly safe.

Nanny's target beam blazed. Jeff saw the rat at the center of the spotlight. The rat lay on its back, the sniffer gripping a rear leg. Blood, black and glistening in the harsh light, stained the sniffer's jaws. It matted the white cuff and flecked the dust in little beads. Ragged trails crisscrossed the dust.

Jeff didn't know why, until the rat strained to sit up. Her front paws flailed, trying to grab the sniffer. The rat lashed at the quivering eyestalks with its teeth. The sniffer jerked backward. The rat collapsed and was dragged. The leg twisted. Then the rat tried again, slower, weaker.

A sound surged out of Jeff. He sprang, and in one bound, landed in front of Nanny. He smashed the gun down as hard as he could on the robot's head. The impact felt like flames on his palms and hammers in his bones. Nanny gripped the gun, ripped it from his grasp, and flung it away.

Jeff stood half bent, hugging his hands tight against his ribs. The terrible sounds were right behind him, feebler now. Jeff shouted, "Make it let go!"

"Naughty boy! Get out of the way."

"No! You've got to stop. They're calling. Orders."

"I have my orders."

"There's an *emergency*!"

The green eye blazed. "I will kill the rat *first*!"

Nanny surged. An arm jabbed, then swung sideways. Jeff dodged. Too slow. It hit him in the ribs, swept him into the air. He hit the wall. His legs crumpled under him.

"*Ow!* Oh! Ow!"

Jeff pushed against the floor to lift his weight off his harshly twisted legs, the searing blister. His left hand touched something cold and rubbery. What?

Nanny asked, "You are hurt?"

"*You* hurt me!"

"Nanny cannot hurt the boy. Nanny protects. Orders." Nanny moved toward him, hesitated—just like it had when he forgot his air mask. He couldn't outfight Nanny, but maybe he could outthink it.

Nanny's eye swiveled to look at the rat. "Priority. Kill the rat."

The rat lay still, front paws splayed to the sides, mouth slack. It breathed, and Jeff acted.

"Oh my leg! My leg! It's broken. Nanny, help, I need help!"

"Decision. Decision." Nanny looked at Jeff. Nanny looked at the rat. Back and forth, regular as a pendulum in an old clock.

At last, power over Nanny. But for how long? Time enough to escape with the rat?

Jeff almost got up, then realized that would show Nanny he'd lied. But if Nanny couldn't see . . .

His hand slid toward the liverwurst, gripped it. When the head glanced away, he lunged and rammed the liverwurst into Nanny's eye. The tube popped. The greasy meat squished between Jeff's fingers as his full weight crashed into Nanny. They went skidding along the floor, a tangle of arms and grippers. Nanny whirled, flinging Jeff into the dust. Then Nanny veered. Nanny bumped into the wall, jittered backward, bumped the wall again. Grippers swiped at the liverwurst.

"Naughty boy! Naughty boy! Naaauuuu—"

There was a pop deep inside Nanny. Electricity arced like swamp lightning all over the black body. Nanny stopped and did not move again.

CHAPTER FIFTEEN

ROUGH BEGINNINGS

When Nanny threw the boy into the air, Rat gave up. She would die. The boy had done his best, but he was only a boy. It felt peaceful to accept her fate. But while she lay there, something more happened. She was not sure what, because she had closed her eyes. She heard a loud pop. She tried to lift her head to see, but that was beyond her strength now. Still she needed to pay attention. Everything was suddenly quiet. Something important had happened.

Even though it would twist her leg, Rat rolled. What an effort that took! It seemed the struggle had taken all the roundness out of her body. But she succeeded. Her leg did not twist. She looked back along her body. For a second Rat stared at the sniffer's bloody jaws gaping like a dead clam. She almost did not understand that she was free.

Her body knew. Up! Move!

Rat found herself on three legs. She wobbled, almost fell, then turned the stumble into motion. Keep going! Rat did not feel any pain, just the heaviness of her useless leg dragging in the dust.

"Don't go! Hey, stop! I can help!"

Rat's legs would not stop. Rat was deep down in her ancient brain seeking dark-ness, wanting aloneness, searching for a little hole.

"Please! Your message. I got it. I won't hurt you!"

Rat looked back over her shoulder. The boy glittered in his silver jumpsuit. His arms were stretched out to her. One hand was covered with brown splotches. More brown was smeared along his leg.

Messy boy!

The friendly thought broke the urge to flee. Rat sagged into the dust. The boy approached. Panic threatened. Rat had vowed never to let human hands touch her again. . . .

Rat smelled liverwurst. But the boy does not like liverwurst. Why was he messy with her liverwurst?

The boy knelt beside her. He did not touch Rat right away. He just looked, his hands resting in his lap. Rat remembered how carefully the boy tended his own blister. His face was full of concern. His clean hand moved toward her.

Let him. Rat fought the urge to bite him. Let him.

The boy stroked Rat very lightly from the tip of her nose to the top of her head. The boy's gentleness unnerved Rat. Her heart surrendered to his touch. With that relaxation the pain came so strongly that Rat lost all awareness of what happened next.

Rat smelled the boy. Not the boy himself, but the boy smell that stayed in his clothes.

Clever boy. He had put Rat in his laundry drawer. Just the safe place she would have picked. Rat stayed curled tight, eyes closed. She could come back to the world slowly, cozy on a used T-shirt.

Rat smelled medicine and tape and bandage. She opened her eyes and looked at her leg. The injured leg did not fit in the close hug of the rest of her body. That was because something stiff was wrapped in with the bandage. She sniffed the end that poked out. It smelled of wood and coffee and the boy. It kept Rat from moving the leg. She did not like that, but there was no pain—amazing after such a terrible thing! She decided to trust the boy. She could always chew the bandage off later.

Rat uncurled and lay on her side. She stretched. Many muscles hurt, but the stretch felt good. She groomed her whiskers, then sniffed—hard, harder. Something was not right!

Fresh air flowed *down* onto Rat in a tiny

stream. Rat looked up. Only a body's length above her was a lid with holes poked in it. Rat twisted onto her paws. The bandaged leg made her rump go lopsided.

Rat saw a rat!

Rat startled. It startled.

That rat *was* Rat, reflected in the clear plastic side of a box. Beyond the reflection Rat saw the boy's room.

Trapped! And out in the open!

Wicked stupid boy!

Rat hobbled to the side. She scrambled against the plastic. Her forepaws got no grip. It hurt, but she stretched up on her hind legs. She pushed at the lid, jostled a crack open.

"Hey! Don't do that." The lid thumped down as the boy rested his hand on it. A fingertip showed in an air hole. "You could fall and hurt yourself."

Hurt *you*! Rat tried to bite the finger. But she could only graze the tight skin with her teeth. Her leg hurt fiercely when she reached so high.

"That tickles," the boy said. He moved his finger away and looked in the side. The box distorted his face, spreading his eyes wide and smearing his features like wet paint.

Tickles! Rat ground her teeth. She meant to draw blood. Put her in a cage! Peer at her like a scientist!

Rat lurched to the side and banged on it with her front paws. Then she signed at the boy with brisk, choppy motions, "Release me at once!"

"Hey! You're talking to me, aren't you? That's sign language, isn't it?"

The boy pressed his eye closer and squinted hard to see Rat's small paws. Rat signed her demand again. The boy stared at her dumbly.

"I don't know sign language."

"Idiot!" signed Rat and turned away. Of course, even if he *did* know sign language, he would not understand Rat. They used a special version in the lab, modified to suit tiny paws.

Rat needed another way to make her demand. She saw an edge of paper in the corner. She raked the T-shirt aside.

"You shouldn't thrash around so much."

Rat pulled the paper out. She made a map in her head. Using her front paws, she moved the paper through her mouth like cloth through a sewing machine. *Nip-nip-nip.* She pressed the nibbled paper against the box. It read: LET ME OUT! NOW!

"Wow!" the boy said. He popped the lid off and reached in. When he tried to slide his hand under her, Rat lunged, catching the loose bit of skin between thumb and forefinger in her teeth. The boy pulled away.

"Yeouch! Those teeth are sharp!" He examined the grazed skin, sliced deep like a paper cut. "Was I doing it wrong? I've never picked up a rat before . . . I mean, an awake one. I hope I didn't hurt you."

Rat shook her head. She felt a little ashamed. She did not threaten to bite when he reached in again. One hand supported her rump, careful not to bend the bandaged leg. The other palm slipped under her belly.

"Is this okay?" It was a very nice, secure hold, but Rat did not respond. "I thought you died when I touched you before. But you had only fainted. Good thing! It probably would have hurt a lot when I set your leg."

Rat was not interested. She jabbed her forepaw at the computer.

"You want to go to the computer?"

Rat nodded and pointed sternly.

The boy limped as he carried Rat to the desk. He held her against his chest. He was very warm, but the open zipper of the jumpsuit rubbed her ribs. Annoying. She was thinking about biting him again, when he set her down gently in front of the keyboard. Rat shivered. She washed a ruffled spot on her shoulder until the fur lay down properly.

Bones filled the computer screen. They were put together in a pattern. Rat read the diagram label: MAMMAL-RODERE-RATTUS-SKELETON. Rat studied the picture. She looked at her forepaw. She wiggled her toes.

"Your bones are different from people bones. I needed to know how to put the splint on. I hope I did a good job."

Rat was not ready to thank the boy. She climbed onto the keys. She tried to get into the proper starting stance, but it was impossible with the hurt leg. She had to use her good back leg and tail to keep from toppling. She could not reach the SHIFT key using only her forepaws. Rat did not like that. It wasn't correct, and she had always been a perfect typist. Besides, it was harder to make the words angry enough without exclamation points. She hit CAPS LOCK and typed: NEVER EVER EVER EVER PUT ME IN A CAGE AGAIN.

"Cage? It's just a box. I thought it would be a safe place while your leg healed. It's busted, you know."

SCIENTISTS USE CAGES. THEY ARE NOT SAFE. FREEDOM IS SAFE.

"That's what you meant! You said you'd never been outdoors! You've been a lab rat! I'm sorry. How could I know?"

How could he know? He couldn't, of course. He did not know anything about Rat.

"You're a Modified, aren't you? And you escaped from somewhere."

Rat nodded.

"I bet you're in big trouble with those scientists, whoever they are. And now you've gotten me in trouble, too. The captain'll kill me when he finds Nanny!"

Rat startled straight up. The hurt leg could not support her. She toppled and slid off the keys.

"Careful!" The boy stopped her from going over the edge. Rat lay on her back, looking into his pale face. Would the captain really kill the boy? Rat remembered the terrible eyes, furious about the stolen food. The captain wanted to kill Rat for that.

"I only meant to blind Nanny so we could get away. But when I hit it with the liverwurst, it went haywire and stopped."

So that was what happened, thought Rat. Her liverwurst had killed the vicious machine. Rat had saved it to eat, but what a better use! Rat wished she could see the robot dead in the dark and the dust.

In the boy's world, destroying Nanny was a mistake. Big enough to bring death? Rat could not be sure. She did not know enough about people. Too many mistakes in the lab, and the black tag got hung on the cage. Next day came the needle full of death. That was animals. But she saw on the news—every day—people killed their own kind, too, in many many ways.

Rat signed, "Will they really punish you with death?"

"It's neat you can do that, but I still don't understand."

How annoying!

Rat rolled and reached for the keys. The boy helped her into position. Even upset he was gentle. The scientists rarely handled Rat as nicely.

LEARN SIGN LANGUAGE SOON. WOULD HE REALLY KILL YOU

"No, silly, but I can't imagine what he will do!"

Relieved, Rat sagged onto the keys. She was glad to know the captain would not hang a black tag on the boy's cabin door.

"Poor rat! You need rest, not problems." His finger stroked Rat's nose, but too quickly, too roughly for comfort. The boy was worried.

Rap-rap-rap.

"Hello in there."

"The captain!" the boy hissed.

Run! Hide!

But Rat could not run. She could not scurry into air vents. Her quick eye saw a shadowy place. Big enough! Most of Rat slipped inside the boy's jumpsuit. The bandage snagged on the zipper.

CHAPTER SIXTEEN

WHERE'S NANNY?

The captain's voice instantly reminded Jeff of the many urgent calls for Nanny while he cared for the rat. Nanny never answered, and now the captain had found out why.

What would he do?

A tickle along his belly made him look down. The rat struggled to get her broken leg into his jumpsuit. He was worrying about the wrong problem! Unsnagging the bandage, he scooped the rat in. She settled along the top of the waistband.

"Jeff?" Mom, too! He jerked the zipper up.

"Is everything okay in there?" And Dad! Everything was not okay. The box sat in plain sight on the bed.

"Ah—wait—I'm not dressed," Jeff called, then crossed the room in three quick strides, hunching over to keep the jumpsuit loose. He flicked the bed covers over the box and sat on the edge of the bed. He tried to sound groggy.

"Okay. Come in."

The door slid open. Jeff stretched and yawned and groaned. He didn't have to fake blinking. It seemed a three-headed monster crowded his doorway. The captain stood in front. Mom and Dad's heads poked over his shoulders. It wasn't an angry monster, and this surprised Jeff. Their expressions were eager, then quickly slumped with disappointment.

"Not here, either," the captain said.

They don't know!

Mom said, "This is terrible! What are we going to do now?"

What was terrible?

The captain asked, "Why aren't you hunting with Nanny?"

"Nanny wouldn't let me."

"But I *ordered* Nanny to take you along."

"Nanny doesn't obey orders," Jeff said. "Nanny *threatened* me when I tried to follow it!"

"Preposterous," the captain said. "Nanny is programmed to *protect* you, to keep you out of trouble, that sort of thing. It couldn't *threaten* you."

Mom said, "It was awfully aggressive about reports, and it did blast that discarded barrel section to pieces right there in the cafeteria. Maybe it's gone vicious or something."

Nanny *was* vicious! Jeff's ribs hurt if he breathed deep. He had bruises. What if he told them that? Would that make wrecking Nanny okay? He wished there had been more time to talk with the rat. The rat was clever. She was sneaky. Maybe they could have come up with a story, like criminals with an alibi. He felt her warm body across his belly, but there was no way to communicate now. He had to figure it out himself.

The captain said to Mom, "Nanny was in hunt mode then—it just needed a target."

"Nanny is in hunt mode *now*!" Mom said.

"Ah . . . right . . ." The captain agreed. Then, considering, he shook his head. "No. It's impossible. There must be some other explanation."

"I don't *need* explanations!" Mom said. Her voice rose. "I need that robot *now*! What are you going to do?"

What could be wrong that they needed Nanny so desperately? Maybe he would *have* to tell. What could he say and stay out of trouble? Jeff was wondering, when he noticed Dad.

While Mom and the captain stood in the door arguing about what to do next, Dad had been observing. Now he stepped toward the computer. Jeff almost gasped. The computer was still on—with rat skeletons and rat words! The words seemed to glow in neon:

NEVER EVER EVER EVER PUT ME IN A CAGE AGAIN.

SCIENTISTS USE CAGES. THEY ARE NOT SAFE. FREEDOM IS SAFE.

Did Dad see them? Jeff willed the screen saver to come on.

Dad picked up the toilet-paper-tube telescope next to the keyboard. Just as Jeff remembered doing, Dad looked in each end. They'd accused him of stealing those lenses. Would Dad remember that?

Dad glanced briefly at Jeff. Jeff couldn't imagine what his own face showed at that moment. Dad puzzled over the three pairs of neat marks. He fingered the charred spot on the tube. Then his eyes turned up to the air vent above the bed.

"Are you listening to me?"

Jeff wrenched his gaze away from Dad, who was lifting the tube to his eye, and looked toward the captain.

"Don't yell at him! This isn't *his* fault," Mom snapped. "Jeff, I know you're always groggy when you wake up, but please pay attention. The captain asked if Nanny told you where it was hunting."

"I don't remember," Jeff said, hating to lie when she was taking his side. "I was mad. Nanny wouldn't let me go. I didn't pay attention. Why do you want to know, anyway? Are we going to die or something?"

"We're scaring you. I'm sorry. I didn't mean to," Mom said. "It's not us, it's the project . . . the *world*! Just the most *senseless* thing has happened! If we don't . . . we'll miss . . . it's just terrible!"

Mom stopped abruptly. She was shaking.

Dad slipped the tube into his pocket and put an arm around her. He said, "One of the meteors damaged a rocket stabilizer somewhere. It's out of control. It keeps jiggling the station." Dad glanced at his watch. "We have four hours and thirty-six minutes to find it and shut it off. Otherwise, we'll miss solar maximum."

Jeff had no idea the critical time for the experiment was so close. He hadn't been paying much attention to his parents lately.

"Only Nanny can work fast enough to find it," the captain said. "There are thousands of those things. We've lost the records on some. Of course, it's one of *those* that's malfunctioning!"

"Sloppy," Mom muttered. Then her fury got the better of her. "I just can't understand how you could be so incompetent!"

"I am *not* listening to that again!" The captain turned like a great blimp and stomped into the hall.

Mom was right behind him, yelling, "Well, just what *are* you going to do? The fate of Earth is at risk here!"

The captain said, "Only if you're right, lady. Otherwise, this is just a royal waste of my time!"

Boots ripped along the corridor.

Mom poked her head in the doorway. Her face was splotchy. "That man! That ignorant man! Please, Jeff. Think *hard*. Any clue, maybe some place you went yesterday . . . *anything* might help. If we don't . . . I mean . . . it'll be another eleven *years* before we can try again. Too late! Those fools will begin global cooling."

She hurried after the captain.

A surge of feeling hit the middle of Jeff's chest. For the first time since arriving here, he wanted to help Mom.

What a mess.

CHAPTER SEVENTEEN

A WARM,
DARK SOFTNESS

When the zipper had gone up, the cloth squeezed tight, squashing Rat hard. It pressed on her body like the sleeve in the lab. They slipped it over you, a stiff ribbed cloth that stank of elastic.

Gotcha!

Can't run!

Can't hide!

It pinned paws flat. It pinched and did not let you move while they did whatever they wanted to you.

Only the angry voices shouting to be let into the room stopped her from scratching at the boy. The captain! The mother! The father! She was helpless. Only the boy could keep her safe.

A lurch. The cloth snatched tighter, hurting her leg.

What is that boy *doing*?

A violent twist. The zipper dug across her back. Then a jounce.

"Okay. Come in."

The boy's voice, heavy with forced tiredness, vibrated against Rat. Clever boy! He was pretending he'd been asleep. Rat heard the door open and a heavy tread. The boy's breath caught.

The boy leaned forward, and Rat missed some things as she adjusted to the sudden roominess. But soon she understood what mattered. They were looking for Nanny. The boy was not telling, not about Nanny, not about Rat.

Rat relaxed into the warm, dark softness of her hiding place. Her body moved with the rhythm of the boy's breath. It was like a lullaby, taking Rat back. Back, back to memories of a time when the fur in her nose was not her fur, the foot in her ear was not her foot, the tail under her chin did not belong to her. Feel the pulse of a dozen hearts different from her own. Smell sweet milk and sour pee and the warm largeness full of goodness.

Such sadness for the long-lost goodness.

Such bliss in the newfound closeness of the boy.

Rat began to knead his T-shirt with her front paws, lost to the passing of time.

Chapter Eighteen
Too Much Attention!

Dad leaned against the desk. At least the screen saver was on now! He took the tube from his pocket. He twirled it thoughtfully.

What did he suspect?

Dad was good at making intuitive leaps on thin evidence. He didn't know about the e-mail, and maybe he hadn't seen or understood the rat's words; but Dad *did* find the wire. He'd seen the tooth marks in neat pairs, just like Jeff.

"Now wasn't that something?" Dad said, looking up at last. "She *yelled* at him."

"Yeah, she did, didn't she?"

"A development." Dad's smile flashed briefly. "Too bad it took circumstances like this. You do realize how serious the situation is, don't you?"

Jeff nodded. He hardly ever lied to his parents, but the damage to Nanny was so bad, and the consequences were so huge, he couldn't find a voice to admit what had happened.

"Imagine! The fate of the world decided by a stray meteor and a missing robot."

Dad looked around. Jeff, too.

So much to hide! He wasn't doing such a great job, either. The mistakes were piling up: the computer left on, the box a big bulge under the blankets, bandages all over the place, the telescope left lying around.

"Are you sure you can't help, Jeff?"

Earlier Jeff had thought there might be a way. But that was before Dad said there were only four hours and thirty-six minutes until solar max. With so little time, what good would it do to tell them where to find a broken robot?

"I can't."

"Hmmm," Dad said. "What happened to your foot?"

Didn't Dad miss *anything*?

"I got a blister from following Nanny halfway around this stupid space station!"

Dropping the tube into his pocket, Dad knelt to inspect Jeff's foot. A little red seeped through the wrapping. At least that could explain all the bloody bandages on the floor.

Dad sniffed. Jeff noticed some liver-wurst still smeared on his jumpsuit leg. How would he explain that?!

Dad sniffed again, then with a little shake of his head, examined the foot.

"Nice job. That's right—you got the first-aid prize at camp last year, didn't you. Bet you'd rather be at camp right now!"

"I guess." Jeff shrugged, then squirmed from a sudden tickle. What was that rat *doing*?

"Oops, did I hurt you?" Dad asked.

"A bit," Jeff lied. He forced his body rigid against the rhythmic push and pull along his left side. The rat was kneading, just like a cat—slow, trancelike. Do rats purr?!

Dad looked at Jeff, a frank, total seeing that made Jeff feel completely noticed—and nervous!

"The rat was here, though, wasn't it?"

Jeff nodded. Lying about the obvious didn't seem smart.

Dad pointed at the vent and asked, "Did you shoot?"

Jeff shook his head. "Nanny."

"Nanny *missed*?"

"Yeah."

"So what actually happened here?"

Jeff told about forgetting the emergency mask and coming back to find the rat. Nothing about the Mid-Ring workshop. Or about the rat standing on the keyboard. He dwelled on Nanny knocking him down and threatening him when he wanted to join the chase. Jeff paused, feeling his terrible anger again as he watched Nanny zip along the corridor, leaving him behind.

What if Nanny had let him come? Would he have killed the rat?

Jeff focused on the warm aliveness inside his clothes. It still seemed lost in some good feeling.

"But Jeff." Dad frowned. He glanced around the room. "Jeff. Where's the gun?"

"Oh no!" Jeff stood straight up. Sharp claws braced deep into his skin. He sat abruptly.

"Oh no . . ."

The sound of excited voices surged in the corridor.

Rip-rip-rip-rip.

The captain had remembered the gun, too.

CHAPTER NINETEEN

Nanny Found

Rat did not mean to dig her claws in. She thought she was in a cozy place, a safe place. Quite a shock, the sudden movement and the fierce pressure when the jumpsuit went taut. The pain awakened in her leg didn't help her think, either.

She almost struggled more, harder, bit, and tore, afraid someone, some*thing* had caught her.

Then there was a jounce and roominess and the sharp, frightened scent rising from the boy.

Rat remembered where she was.

She felt the boy groan from deep in his chest. "Oh no . . ."

Something's happened!

She forced herself still.

Good thing.

The next sound she heard was the captain saying, "Where's that gun?"

The scent of the boy's fear grew so strong, Rat had to fight against a sympathetic panic herself. The smell spoke to her instincts. Run! Escape! Hide!

"I—ah—I—"

"Don't bother," the captain said. "Control? Locate the boy's gun immediately."

"Jeff! You didn't *shoot* Nanny?"

The father's voice blared into Rat's ears. He must be very close! Where are the other adults? Her teeth started to grind together. She clenched her mouth tight. The father might be close enough to hear!

"He couldn't have," the captain said. "The SmartGun was programmed only to shoot rats."

Wicked gun! Wicked man!

Beep. "Captain, we have a signal from the gun. It appears to be in the Mid-Ring workshop."

"What do you mean 'appears'? Is it there or isn't it?"

Beep. "The maps say there's no air in the workshop, so I don't understand how it *could* be there."

"Well?"

The boy flinched. "There's air."

"And when we find that gun, we'll find Nanny, right?"

The boy nodded.

"Jeff?" the mother said. "You *lied* to us?"

"I didn't mean to. I had to save the rat."

"Save—the—rat?"

"I was going to kill it, to protect the project, to help. Then Nanny wouldn't even let me hunt. I followed anyway. When I got there, a sniffer had it and there was all this blood . . . and this *sound* . . . I *had* to save it. But Nanny wouldn't stop. I only meant to blind Nanny. Something happened . . . and now everything's ruined. I'm sorry."

His body trembled. He was upset, but not blubbering. The muscles across his stomach were tight and hard like steel. Confessing, yes, but with control, saying nothing about Rat. What a good boy!

"What—*what* happened to Nanny?" the captain asked. "Spit it out!"

Somehow Rat must save him from that brutal man.

"I destroyed it!"

"More lies!" the captain scoffed. "Nanny can fight soldiers! You couldn't even scratch it!"

"I'm *not* lying! Nanny's dead!"

"Jeff, are you sure?" asked the father.

"There was this big crack, big ball of electricity. Nanny stopped and stayed stopped. I guess that's all I really know."

"This is incredible—" the mother said. "A . . . *rodent*? Nanny . . . dead? I want to wake up now."

Rat began to understand. This was only a little bit about Nanny. Mostly it was about the project. Vaguely Rat recalled the talk before all this excitement about the gun. They needed Nanny to fix something. What? Rat had stopped paying attention.

"You were fighting with Nanny?" the father asked.

"I *told* Nanny to stop. I told it Control was calling. It wouldn't obey. It *attacked* me!"

"This is very serious . . . if true," the captain said. "Control! Send the chief engineer and a repair crew to the workshop immediately!"

Beep. "Yes, sir."

"Move out, all of you!" the captain ordered. "To the workshop. We'll get to the bottom of this right now."

The boy went stiff. Rat startled.

If he stood up, Rat might be discovered!

How could Rat save herself? She couldn't even run!

She could bite.

She could slash.

Rat flexed her toes. Slowly, quietly she rubbed her teeth together to make the edges sharp.

They would be sorry if they found Rat!

"He can't," the father said. "His foot is hurt."

"Hurt?" the mother said. "There's *blood*!"

The boy shifted. Cloth crinkled. The mother must be looking at the foot. That close! Rat tried to fit even flatter to the boy's body. Maybe he liked that, because the clenched muscles loosened some.

"Look at this! Look! You told us he'd be safe with Nanny!"

"I don't understand," the captain said.

"Oh, Nanny didn't—" the father began to explain.

Beep. "Captain, we're in the workshop."

The boy's breath caught. The adults', too. Rat could not hear anyone breathing.

Beep. "We've found the gun. Looks like the kid's been hitting rocks with it. What's that? Okay, Tom sees Nanny. Hold on."

Beep. "It's . . . *yuck* . . . smeared with . . . *liverwurst* . . . and quite dead. A massive power surge by the looks."

"*Liverwurst!*"

Rat licked her lips. She would like some liverwurst.

Beep. "All *over* the place. . . . It's impossible, but wait a minute—I'm taking the head off. Blast it! The stuff squished through and shorted the power-phase integrator. We must've nicked the O-ring seal putting Nanny back together."

They hadn't done it, the captain had. Jeff remembered how he had been hurrying and dropped Nanny's head. It clattered in the opening, then the captain smacked it down tight with his big fist. And after all those times yelling at Jeff for running, too.

"This is unbelievable!" the mother said. "The world is going to freeze because of . . . of *liverwurst?*"

"Can you fix it?" the captain asked.

Beep. "Don't know, sir. Even if Nanny's

165

brain survived, the body's wrecked. Days, weeks maybe—"

"Give me that radio!" the mother yelled. "We don't have days! *Please* . . . we need that stabilizer fixed now!"

Rat knew that word. The label she had read so painstakingly in the dim light popped back into her head: STABILIZER ROCKET #724 CONTROL BOX.

The mysterious noise! From behind the big metal box with the little blue light. The one the meteor smashed. Rocket exhaust!

Rat could save the project.

Help scientists?

"Janice . . . shhhh . . . here, give that radio back to the captain."

"Oh, Greg . . . we'll be too late!"

"Do your best, chief," the captain said.

Beep. "Aye, sir."

The voices were all far away. They were not paying attention to the boy. Rat must act now. She had no idea if they would ever leave him alone in time. But how to tell him?

Did he know Morse code?

She could not waste the time finding out.

She shimmied up his T-shirt. The boy leaned forward, maybe thinking she needed more room. His skin felt hot and soft against her toes. Sensitive. Good.

Slowly she drew "724" across his stomach.

He started to squirm, then went very still.

She drew "724" again.

"T two four?" the boy whispered into his collar. His hot breath washed over Rat.

She nipped him. Pay attention!

"Ow!"

Noisy boy! A rat would never yelp at such a little nip.

"Jeff, what's the matter?"

"Ah, um, my blister . . . it smarted suddenly."

Rat scratched the "7" again, not gently.

"Owww . . . ohhhhh! *Seven* two four." He spoke out loud.

Hasty boy! He did not wait for the other clue.

CHAPTER TWENTY

Some Advice

The captain snapped, "What's that supposed to mean?"

"I . . . I don't know."

They stared at him.

"Then what did you say it for?"

Come on, rat! Help!

"Did you remember something?" Mom asked. "Is that something Nanny told you?"

Great cover, if he ever figured out what it meant.

"Uh . . . um . . ." He tapped his forehead, pretending to think, buying time. The toenails touched his skin again, but moved more gently.

RS724.

Jeff didn't know what that meant. How could he let the rat know he needed more information? A stomach only worked one way!

TELL.

Jeff felt the command firmly etched just above his belly button. He obeyed, even though it made no sense to him.

"Um . . . R-S-seven-two-four?"

"That's a stabilizer designation!" The captain turned to Jeff's computer. Keys clicked under his pounding fingers.

Mom asked, "When did Nanny say that?"

"Err . . . I'm not sure—"

"Garbage!" the captain said, scowling at the map on the screen. "That stabilizer's been deactivated for decades."

Dad said, "And there was no air in the Mid-Ring workshop, remember?"

The captain straightened at the computer. He smacked the CLEAR button, venting, "Useless!" as he grabbed for his radio. "Control! Get me a real-time status on RS724. Now!"

"I can't *stand* this!" Mom clenched her hands together and pressed them hard against her lips.

They all stared at the radio, shaking in the captain's grasp.

Beep. "Operational, sir! Random power spikes. It's firing!"

"Kill it!"

Jeff chewed his lip . . . one . . . two . . . three . . .

Beep. "Done. We're showing station stability!"

"Make sure it stays that way!"

Beep. "Yes, sir!"

"Jeff!" Mom practically squealed. She hugged him. Jeff braced, expecting to feel rat scratches in protest. Then over his shoulder, Mom saw her watch.

"Oh no, we're not ready!" Mom started to pull away, half turning toward the door, then stopped herself. She held Jeff at arm's length. For a moment the glittering hardness of anticipation left her eyes. Jeff felt hugged in every cell of his body. "You're wonderful. Gotta run."

"Run?!" Jeff said. "You don't know how."

Mom laughed, a real belly burst. "Teach me when this is all over, okay?"

Jeff nodded. "Good luck, Mom."

"Captain, I need your full cooperation immediately! Greg!" She hurried out the door waddling as fast as she dared.

The captain hesitated. His expression showed he didn't think Jeff was so wonderful. "You're confined to quarters until I figure all this out. Understood?"

"Yes, sir."

"That's harsh," Dad said when the captain left. "You going to be okay on your own?"

"Have been so far."

"Ouch." Dad winced. "Okay, that's fair. But you understand, things can't change for a while?"

Jeff nodded. He didn't want any more attention right now.

"Good. I'd better run—I mean, waddle. When things calm down, I'll make it up to you. We'll spacewalk to the moon or something."

Jeff smiled. "Thanks, Dad."

"Take a nap. You look beat. I'll check in on you before we hit solar max." Dad paused at the door. "Um, what happened to the rat?"

Jeff was ready for that question. Even while confessing about destroying Nanny, a part of him remained untouched by the stress; cold, clear, certain he would never, never tell them the full story.

"It got away."

Dad's right eyebrow arched, the way it did when they played chess and Jeff made an unexpected move.

"Ah. Well then, best keep this out of sight." Dad tossed the tube telescope to Jeff.

CHAPTER TWENTY-ONE
A New Nest

Gzzzzriiiiiiip—down came the zipper. The jumpsuit went slack. Rat rolled onto her back in the cozy pouch that formed in his lap. The boy stared down at her. His eyes glittered, glassy and unseeing. The dark shadows of fatigue rimmed them. His mouth moved a few times before he actually spoke.

"Talk about the Inquisition! I never lied so much in my whole life!"

So what? We escaped, thought Rat. Be calm. Be happy.

Rat squirmed. She found a curious little dimple in the boy's belly—just the right size for poking a nose into!

"Hey!" The boy jerked, laughed.

Rat did it again.

"Stop!" He flopped onto his back, giggling. Tricky for Rat, not to fall off as he tried to wiggle the little dimple away from her persistent nose.

"Enough! Oh, please, stop! Ouch—"

Rat had trampled on his scratches. She slid off onto the blanket.

The boy caught his breath, then sat up. He pulled up his T-shirt. "Look at me!"

A long, ugly bruise left by Nanny's gripper. Pink scratches. Three claw punctures. And a nip. Tiny beads of blood here and there.

"Sorry," signed Rat.

"What?"

Bother! She must teach him sign language right away. She did not want to leave the comfortable bed for the cold, hard keyboard.

She didn't have to worry. The boy limped over to the cubbies. Returning, he placed the first-aid kit, a couple packets of super-concentrated rations, and his pocket computer next to Rat.

Clever boy!

"I'm starving! You, too?"

Rat nodded. Food would be nice!

He broke off an inch of the leathery ration stick for Rat and stuffed the rest into his mouth. Rat nibbled. Much tastier than the long-lost food pellets, but still not as good as liverwurst.

"I wonder if confined to quarters means I can't go to the cafeteria?"

Rat certainly hoped not!

"I'd almost be happy to see Nanny show up with some milk and cookies."

Rat agreed.

The boy took off his jumpsuit and T-shirt. He knelt by the bed and opened the first-aid kit. He dabbed disinfectant over the scrapes and punctures . . . wincing and drawing sharp breaths as he did so.

Rat turned on the pocket computer. She typed, SORRY ABOUT THE HURTS.

Rat liked the little keys so close together.

"I wouldn't mind if you had *chewed* those numbers into my skin! How did you know, though?"

CONTROL BOX NEAR NEST. METEOR SMASHED IT.

"A meteor hit your nest? *That* must've been scary!"

Rat just nodded. She did not have the energy to tell him how the decompression nearly killed her, how she escaped only to be caught by the sniffer. Horrible! If the boy hadn't come . . .

The boy looked at Rat with sympathetic eyes.

"We've had some close calls. And the captain's still mad. It doesn't matter. I have to live with Mom, not him!"

He tended the last of the scratches. Sweat pearled along the line of his upper lip as he worked. Rat sniffed, scenting the saltiness.

"Have I got bad breath or something? Oh, I know! You're *learning* things, aren't you?" He poked his nose close to Rat's nose. He sniffed.

SILLY BOY!

He smiled and stroked her nose. Rat nudged the finger behind her ear. He scratched. She hunched her shoulder so that the itchy scarred spot fell under his finger. Her lip curled, and her right eye went squinty.

Oooooooo! She wanted him to rub her all over. She wanted to curl up in his healing warmth and sleep.

"Hey, what's your name? You never said."

I AM RAT.

"Rat? Huh. Okay, Rat, how about a nap?"

Rat nodded, then held up her paw. He had forgotten something.

FATHER RETURNING.

"Oh, right. I think Dad's on our side. I think he guessed. He saw the tube with your teeth marks. It might be okay if he saw you."

NO NO NO. Rat hit the keys hard, making the small computer bounce on the bed. She was not ready to trust the father. Yes, he behaved oddly . . . noticing and not saying. But what did he *really* think? Rat did not know. The boy did not know. The boy was hasty, not careful like Rat. She must teach him, or the way ahead might not be all liverwurst and soft T-shirts.

SAFEST SECRET.

The boy nodded. "I'll lock the door."

OPEN LAUNDRY DRAWER.

"Huh? Oh! So you can roll into it and hide. Good thinking. Wouldn't want to do the jumpsuit again."

The boy pulled the drawer open about a foot. He moved Rat to the pillow. While the boy cleared the box and other things off the bed, Rat trampled a welcoming hollow. He locked the door, grabbed another pillow, then slipped under the covers.

Quiet and dim. Rat liked that. But sleep did not come easily. She could feel the heat of the boy. Smell the stale fear lingering on his skin. Hear his breath. So loud! Though growing shallower, quieter. She had yearned to share her nest again, but with a human boy?

The boy drew a deep breath and spoke. "You know, Rat, it'll take Mom and Dad about two weeks to collect the data they need. There'll be time to do all those things we talked about in our e-mail—like play chess. And if the captain ever lets me out, I can take you to the zero-g room. I bet that'll feel good on your leg. Then when it's time for us to leave, I'll smuggle you home with me. Won't that be super?!"

Go back to Earth? That had seemed impossible before. But with the boy, maybe she could. Would she make the trip in his jumpsuit?

Yes, Rat thought, *that* would be the way. Snuggle me—smuggle me. Take me to grass. And dirt. What a marvelous boy!

Rat stretched and wiggled until her nose reached across to his pillow. She nibbled his earlobe.

"I guess that means you like the idea."

Yes. Yes. Rat nodded. She would go back to Earth with this boy who smelled nice and had saved her life.

She curled her sharp nails against the soft, pink pads of her forepaw. With her knuckles, she lightly traced "GN" on his cheek.

"What? GN? Oh, good night, right? Good night, Rat."

MICHAEL J. DALEY has enjoyed a lifelong love of science, spaceships, and science fiction. He writes his stories on a solar-powered laptop in a five-foot-by-five-foot-square tower room. This keeps him well acquainted with the cramped conditions in spaceships and space stations! When not traveling the stars, Mr. Daley lives in Westminster, Vermont, with his wife, children's author Jessie Haas.